"This is Thunderdome, and Death's Listening. He'll take the first man who screams..."

Aunty Entity has risen to her feet, and the crowd's restless murmur had hushed once more. Her voice was like a benediction. Then she raised her hands.

At her signal the Guards let go of the two men, heaving them back toward the center of the arena with a rough shove.

Suspended on his cable, his movements completely out of his control, Max sailed toward Blaster. Their bodies slammed together with a teeth-jarring "thud" and rebounded. Blaster arced forward again, completely in control at the end of his own rope. His huge open hand smacked into the side of Max's head, twirling him like a top. Blaster smacked Max again, set him spinning faster.

The arena flashed past in a nauseating blur. Giddy with vertigo, tasting blood, Max saw Blaster's helmet blink past again and heard the giant's inhuman, echoing laughter. It was a nightmare in zero gravity . . . there were no rules at all, just like he had been promised—not even the rules of nature . . .

MAD MAX
BEYOND THUNDERDOME

A novelization by Joan D. Vinge

Based on the screenplay by
Terry Hayes and George Miller

WARNER BOOKS

A Warner Communications Company

WARNER BOOKS EDITION

Copyright © 1985 by Warner Bros. Inc. and Kennedy Miller
Productions Pty. Ltd.
All rights reserved.

Warner Books, Inc.
666 Fifth Avenue
New York, N.Y. 10103

 A Warner Communications Company

Printed in the United States of America

First Printing: July, 1985

10 9 8 7 6 5 4 3 2 1

CHAPTER 1

AMBUSH IN THE DESERT OF DESPAIR

They called it the Desert of Despair. It had had another name, or two or three, back when there were still maps and anyone who cared what was written on them. This was the name that stuck, because it still had some meaning. Nothing moved on its mirage-haunted surface for endless miles except the red, restless sand, creeping grain on grain toward some nameless destination. It had lain unchanging for centuries, millennia . . . unlike the world around it, which had changed, and changed again, until nuclear war had put an end to everything but desolation.

The wind sighed and circled above the wastes, probed the sandblasted skull of a dead boar half buried in a dune, whistling a funeral dirge through its empty snout and hollow eye sockets. Forever dissatisfied, the wind swept on, rising toward the mass of ancient rocks and cliffs that lay far to the north, a jumble of red sandstone stitched with the fragile green of vegetation. The hills rose like great blisters from the burned, feverish flatlands, the only feature with any measurable height for as far as eyes could see, if any eyes were watching.

If any eyes were watching, they would have seen the rattletrap relic that had once been a single-engine plane soar out over the cliffs, as incongruous as a pterodactyl. It circled down and down through the erratic currents of heated air, searching endlessly, restlessly, like the scavenger wind.

In the cockpit Jedediah sat at the controls, his bloodshot eyes insectoid behind Coke-bottle-bottom glasses, a pith helmet pulled down over his ears—an explorer of the New Age, searching for that rarest of finds, live prey.

"There!" a boy's voice cried in his ear.

He looked over at Jedediah, Jr., his extra set of eyes and hands, saw where his son's hand was pointing. A small plume of dust was rising unmistakably into the air, far below and still far ahead across the desert. Jedediah let out a braying whoop of laughter and pushed forward on the control stick. The plane dove like a carrion bird, dropping down again, slowly overtaking the telltale marker of dust. As he began to make out detail, Jedediah cut the motor; the sound of his engine could carry for miles across the empty desert. The propeller slowed, flickering to a stop. All that they could hear now was the wind rushing past. "Take the controls," he said to the boy.

Far below, all that the driver of the camel train heard was wind . . . it was virtually all he had heard for weeks, besides the grunting of the camels and his own voice. He straddled the engine block of a derelict off-road vehicle, swathed from head to foot in loose black robes, a post-apocalyptic bedouin. Only his eyes were visible, and he would have covered them, too, if there was any way. He squinted into the glare and dust, watching the swaying humps of the eight camels hitched to the dune buggy's corpse, dragging it with infinite patience toward his destination. After so long alone in the heat and silence, watching the same horizon, the same hypnotic motion, day after day, he could almost forget that anyone else existed in the world, that they would hijack what he had before they would offer to trade. . . . The part of his mind that never forgot had long ago given up searching the sky for danger.

The back of his makeshift wagon, its armored cage covered by a jury-rigged canopy of tarp, was loaded down with the goods of a survivor's trade: bundles of firewood, blackened pots and pans, mufflers and piping ripped from other gutted vehicles, sacks of miscellaneous junk; anything somebody somewhere might possibly want and be willing to trade for something he wanted. There was even the intact radiator of a truck. He figured to make a good profit off of it someday. Although if anyone had asked him what he wanted in return, he would have been hard-pressed to answer.

He grunted as the caravan bumped down into the plain of a dry riverbed; slapped mechanically at the eternal retinue of flies that followed the camels, to suck their blood and his. Slung from his wrist was a flyswatter, a piece of bright plastic lashed to a sturdy wooden shaft. He called it his Lifesaver.

One of the two mangy goats tied to the rear of the truck bleated unexpectedly. The driver glanced back and then up, caught in a sudden premonition. He gaped.

A single-engine aircraft was bearing down on him out

of the empty sky. His mouth fell open in disbelief, all the reaction he had time for before the swooping plane's dropped wheel smashed into the side of his face and knocked him sprawling headfirst out of his seat. He struck the ground hard and rolled; struggled up, trying to get his feet under him . . . collapsed again, gasping. On his hands and knees in the sand, he raised his head; his ringing ears filled with the roar of a plane's engines as the hijackers buzzed his caravan a second time. Forcing his eyes to focus, he saw someone hanging from the airplane's wing as it dropped lower and lower.

In the plane's cockpit, Jedediah, Jr. peered out, guesstimating airspeed and angle of attack. "Bombs away!" he shouted gleefully. His father let go of the plane's undercarriage and dropped squarely onto the backpack of the startled lead camel. He grabbed up its reins and dug his booted heels into its ribs. "Go on! Giddyup!" he bellowed. The camel, half crazed with terror and surprise, bawled and broke into a shambling run. The rest of the team followed, catching its frenzy, dragging the dune buggy and the bleating goats forward at a gallop. Jedediah, clinging to the camel's back like a burr, laughed in wild triumph; his hyena laughter pelted like stones on the head of the driver, still on his knees in the dust, rapidly being left behind.

The driver staggered to his feet, glancing up into the sky for the length of a heartbeat in dazzled disbelief, as the airplane soared away again toward the distant hills. The blazing sand began to burn the soles of his bare feet; he cursed himself for taking off his boots while he rode. And then he turned back, his fists knotted and his eyes deadly. He'd been goddamn careless . . . but he wasn't stupid. He started to run.

Jedediah turned to look back as he rode, saw the plane

already no more than a speck, safely out of range. And in the nearer distance, the driver running like hell after him through the cloud of choking sand. He drove his boot heels into the camel's sides again; it lunged forward with a new burst of speed, the rest of the train thundering after it.

The driver, watching his caravan and everything he owned begin to pull away from him, put on a fresh burst of speed. Winning or losing this race meant the difference between life and death. . . . Half blinded by the dust, his breath coming in ragged gasps, he began to gain on the caravan again.

The dune buggy's canopied rear end emerged slowly from the cloud of dust as he gained ground inch by agonizing inch. As he began to see the shadowed, junk-filled interior clearly, a monkey's small, round, terrified face suddenly appeared in the opening. *Christ, the monkey*— The monkey was the only thing in the world he gave a damn about. Animals were the only creatures he trusted in this godforsaken wilderness . . . and that monkey trusted him. The monkey leaped up and down, shrieking with distress, urging him on. Up ahead the hijacker was flogging the stampeding camels to even greater effort; the monkey caromed off the walls, still crying in shrill panic. The driver ran on and on, the back of the wagon barely beyond his outstretched hand now. . . . One yard . . . half a yard . . . He reached out, straining with the last of his strength, the monkey's shrieks loud in his ears. *Almost . . . almost . . .*

The rear of the buggy began to pull away again, eluding him by agonizing inches . . . feet . . . yards.

The driver's outstretched hand dropped; his run slowed to a shambling trot, a jog, a walk. He stood still, his chest heaving, his raw feet stained red with dust and blood. He

stood and watched his entire world disappear into a cloud
of dust; suddenly dizzingly aware of the pain in his feet,
his chest, his aching head. Furious with frustration, he
slapped the flyswatter hard on his calf.

In the back of the dune buggy the monkey still clung to
the tarp, silent now as it watched the lone figure growing
smaller moment by moment in the desert's pitiless
immensity. And then, in sudden frenzy or inspiration, it
picked up a battered pot and hurled it out the back of the
buggy and into the sand. Another pan followed, plates,
bottles—anything and everything the monkey could get
its small, leathery hands on—spun out of the buggy,
leaving a trail of detritus behind, littering the shimmering landscape with debris.

Blissfully unsuspecting, its kidnapper rode on toward
the horizon, his hooting, lunatic laughter echoing out
over the desert again as the dune buggy disappeared from
the driver's sight over a distant rise.

The driver stood where he was, panting, staring at the
glittering arrow of jettisoned goods lying between the
rutted tire tracks with bleak eyes. And then he began to
walk again, doggedly following the trail, stooping to pick
up his random possessions as he went. He stopped again
after a few yards and turned to look back. Far above and
very far behind him now, the skeletal plane was swooping
and soaring in triumph above the jumbled red-rock cliffs.
He heard the distant purr of its motor, and maybe only in
his mind, a high, mocking echo of the hijacker's laughter.
He stared a moment longer, paralyzed by that vision of a
lost world, by the last sight he would have of the first
airplane that he had seen in over fifteen years . . . marking its destination indelibly in his brain.

Looking down again, he dropped the few items he had
already collected into the sand and began to unwind his

turban. It occurred to him that he was lucky he'd had it on when he was hit, or the blow from the plane's wheel would have cracked his skull like an egg instead of simply leaving him with a knot like a baseball on the side of his head. He didn't like continuing on bare-headed, but he needed something to carry his salvaged belongings. He pulled the last of the windings free, exposing his face and head to the sun's merciless heat, staring out across the empty wastes as he began to knot it into a sack.

His brown hair, which he had once kept cut short with almost military precision, was shoulder-length now, streaked with gray at the temples. He was nearing middle age, and the life he had led aged a man fast. Two days' growth of stubble stood out on his lean jaw. A white scar slashed starkly across his sun-browned forehead and cheek, angling down over his left eye. The eye itself was as startlingly blue as the desert sky; he had nearly lost it in the fight. He was still alive; the man who had marked him was not.

They called him Mad Max, if they called him anything. Names in the new order were totem signs, no longer simple markers for a face. Markers were for tombstones. Once he had had a name, just like the blister mountains shimmering in the heat haze behind him ... just like everyone else. Max Rockatansky. But that had been half a lifetime ago, before the apocalypse, when names and life itself had still seemed to have some meaning ... before his country had been blown to hell along with the rest of the world, before all of humanity had become a victim of its own venality, stupidity, and greed. Max had survived nearly half a lifetime since then, largely because in the depths of his soul he didn't give a damn whether he lived or died.

But surviving got to be a habit in time. And he was

damned if he was going to die like this, leaving that human hyena who'd 'jacked his goods to spit on his memory and call him an easy mark. Revenge was as good a motivator as anything he knew . . . and he knew it better than most.

He stuffed the salvaged goods into his makeshift pack and began to walk again, limping now from the pain of his cut and blistered feet, from the chronic ache of an old wound in his knee. The brace he had made for his leg, hidden beneath his robes, squeaked faintly as he walked. Farther along the caravan's trail he found a water bottle. It wasn't very heavy. He shook it, feeling the liquid slosh inside. Not even half full. He slung it at his back and kept walking. After a few more yards he found one boot, and then the other. He pushed them onto his feet with silent gratitude. If nothing else, he was going to find the thief and get his monkey back. Even after all these years some things didn't change. Max paid his debts.

Farther down the track he found the last of the monkey's legacy . . . a small whistle, a thing like a pipe with a leering skull face carved on it. He put it to his lips almost absently and blew. The skull emitted an eerie, high-pitched screech, whistling through its teeth. The sound echoed away across the wilderness, mournful and haunted, fleeting like a ghost toward the distant hills.

Max hung the whistle from its thong around his neck and trudged on in silence.

CHAPTER 2

BARTERTOWN

Four days later the caravan's trail joined what passed for a real road, the cracked and sandblasted remains of something that had once been paved highway . . . running now from Nowhere to Nowhere. Max stepped onto the road, grateful for easier going, walking with a mindless, shambling stride, his thoughts purposely empty. He followed the road as the sun followed its track across the sky, letting time and space flow past him with grim indifference.

The sudden darkness of shadow fell across his track as unexpectedly as a pit. He stopped, gazing blankly at the line of darkness for a long moment. And then he looked up again, squinting. A signpoint stood before him like a grave marker, at the place where a number of tracks converged with this one. Nailed to the upright post were several gray, splintered slats of wood, each one pointing in a different direction. On each of the markers was the name of a different great city, the symbols of a vanished civilization.

SYDNEY, he read, 500 KM. TOKYO, 5600 KM. NEW YORK, 9800 KM. MOSCOW . . . He stopped reading. Each of the signs had been crossed out in black paint with equal black humor. Only one name remained, splashed across the pile of rocks that supported the signpost's base. A jagged arrow pointed toward BARTERTOWN. A nest of snakes lay on the baking-hot surface of the rocks, studying him with slitted eyes. As he watched, one of them slithered down and away.

Max's cracked lips twitched with an unreadable grimace. That answered his question. He started on, turning with the arrow, squinting into the sunset. Bartertown was where he was heading. . . .

A gibbous moon rose as the sun set, filling the black, star-strung emptiness of the night sky like an immense Japanese lantern. Max walked all night, taking advantage of its light and the merciful absence of the sun. He had not eaten since he had lost the camels and the truck; he had been out of water for two days. The odds were getting poor that he would make it through another day of this heat. He hoped that the road to Bartertown ran out before his strength did. The ground was rougher now, the trail climbing bare, stony hills and dropping down into steep gullies, forcing him to do the same.

At last, just as dawn was breaking, he climbed one more rise and stopped. An iguana lay dozing on a rock at his feet. He considered killing it and eating it. But as he looked around for a stone he glanced out over the rise and down. Beyond and below stretched a vast plain, bordered on one side by the dazzling expanse of a huge salt lake. The early-morning sun made the dry lake bed glitter like a bed of broken glass. The image suited. Conditions on a salt lake were so forbidding, the heat so intense that they made the desert he had just come through seem like the Garden of Eden. The lake bed was called the Devil's Anvil by the people of the town below.

The town below. Shimmering like a vision in the heat haze that hugged the lakeshore lay the pit of what had once been an open-cut mine, nested in the man-made crater of what had once been a hill. Now it was home to several thousand people . . . a major metropolis by post-holocaust standards. *Bartertown.* Three dust-fogged roads and a dead railway line bisected the plain below, all converging on the town. Already trudging along the roads from all directions were a ragtag collection of survivors, all bringing in goods to trade. Max licked his parched lips, his hands tightening. He had reached his journey's end. Now all he had to do was find the man who had gotten there first with his possessions.

Max scrambled down the hillside, one more survivor heading toward the oasis of civilization below. Half an hour later, he halted beneath the massive sign suspended on a high metal framework at the town's entrance. He looked up.

BARTERTOWN

HELPING BUILD A BETTER TOMORROW

His mouth quirked. He started on, letting himself be absorbed into the motley mass of traders slowly making their way beneath the sign. He glanced around him as he walked, studying his companions, his senses coming to life again after the sensory deprivation of his time in the desert. Adrenaline spilled into his bloodstream, startling

his numbed mind and body into alertness; the presence of
so many human beings at once, after so long, set his
nerves jangling. A crowd was danger—an uncontrollable
situation, too many alternatives, jaws full of teeth waiting
to swallow up an unwary man. But this was where the
thief had come, and so it was where he belonged, for now.

He passed two grizzled middle-aged men who had
yoked themselves together like draft animals to drag a
clumsy wooden cart into town. In its bed lay the blackened remains of an aircraft engine. Farther on he passed
two men armed to the teeth and riding on ponies, driving
a herd of livestock to market. Their stock, tethered
together, included several scrawny goats and cows and
several men with shaven heads in bedraggled yellow
robes. The men chanted tonelessly as they stumbled
along: "Hare   Krishna ... Hare   Krishna ... Hare
Hare ... Hare Rama ... "

Max wondered dimly whether he was seeing the last
Hare Krishnas on Earth. God knew he had seen everything else by now. Passing the men, he found a pair of
women shackled in front of them. One of the women was
extremely fat; the other was slender and beautiful, like a
porcelain figurine—and as fragile. Frail and trembling,
she moved as if every step she took might be her last.
Max looked away hastily. *Everything.*

On the road ahead a multicolored miniature umbrella
bobbed above the crowd like a beach ball carried on the
tide. It was perched hatlike over the skull of a pinch-
faced vendor loaded down with bottles and cups until he
looked like a refugee court jester. He stood in the traces
of a cart loaded with a large metal tank, calling out in a
nasal drone to the passersby: "Water ... water ... get it
here. It's the real thing, not Coke"—his rubber face
twisted into a smile—"it's water. . . ." *Civilization.* As

Max watched, thirsty travelers stopped to buy a cupful and gulp it down.

Max moved closer, his eyes riveted now on the shining liquid flowing freely into cup after cup. He swallowed and swallowed again.

"Water," the water seller called, still grinning. "Nature's special . . . no added sugar . . . no preservatives . . . pure water. Official drink of the Twenty-fifth Olympics . . . water. . . ." An empty wooden birdcage hanging from a stick jutted up past his shoulder. He looked around as Max drew closer, parched and sunburned, a sure bet for at least a quart.

The water seller's grin widened. "Step up, schmuck," he said congenially, "let's get some dealing done. H-two-oh, that's my go. . . ."

Too easy . . . Max looked away with an effort and kept walking. The water seller hauled his cart around, starting after him, keeping pace as he kept up the diarrhea of words. "What ya got? Bullets? Medicine? Smoke? A block of chew?"

Max shook his head, still walking.

"Don't you understand?" The water seller pushed in front of him, stopping him in his tracks. "This is water. You can't live without it. . . ." Lifting a canteen, he poured a stream of clear liquid into a marked beaker, watching Max like a hawk. This sucker didn't have much on him worth trading, but he looked like he ought to be willing to trade his own blood for water, the shape he was in. "Tell you what—one pint, two joints. . . ." He waved it under Max's nose.

Max stared at him, swallowing again until his voice worked. "You drink it," he said hoarsely.

The water seller laughed, impressed. "You're cautious—I like that. But it could take days to poison a man. . . ." He reached into a hidden inner pocket of his coat and dragged out a canary. "On the other hand, one of these little birdies . . ." Squeezing the bird's beak open, he poured a trickle of water down its throat. He pushed the bird gently into the cage hanging above his shoulder and watched it flutter around. "See?" Still the stranger hesitated. He grinned in exasperation, lifting a hand, holding out the beaker to Max again. "Avoid the Christmas rush. One pint for two smokes."

Max reached into the folds of his loose outer robe. The water seller stiffened as what looked like a gun appeared in the stranger's hand, pointing straight at his own chest. But Max only moved its barrel until it hovered close to the beaker of water. The thing that looked like a weapon began to chatter frantically. An explosion of laughter burst out of the water seller as he realized that all the stranger held was a Geiger counter. "What's a little fallout?" he said.

Max turned away wordlessly and walked on.

"Have a nice day." This time the water seller did not follow. He'd lost the sale, but at least that was all he'd lost. Still grinning, he turned back, eyeballing the next trader coming down the road. "Water . . . water . . ." he called. "It's the real thing. Water . . ."

Max glanced back once, saw the trader stop, fumbling in his pocket. He handed over a couple of cartridges, and the water seller gave him the beaker. He drank it down greedily. Max looked ahead again.

Rising before him now was the strangest sight he had seen in a long time. An old tunnel bored into the steep side of the hill. Once it had serviced the mine inside; now, defended by a heavy iron grille and armed guards, it gave the only access to Bartertown. He could see nothing of the town inside the heart of the rock, only the tunnel's fanged and gaping maw, thick with eerie shadows cast up along its walls by the mismatched assortment of industrial lights strung overhead. He couldn't remember when he had last seen so many lights—functioning electric lights—all burning; he wondered where they got the fuel for that much power. The air was choked with dust and smoke, further obscuring his view of the promised land hidden in the moutain ahead.

But sitting inside a booth cut from the rock wall just at the tunnel's entrance was a fee collector, passing judgment on the worth of the traders who came to the gates. The apocalypse, or at least Bartertown, had plainly been good to him; his epicene, leather-aproned body was big and flabby, his skin soft and pink.

Max waited his turn in line behind a trapper whose cart was piled high with animal pelts and carcasses. The Collector leaned forward in his battered armchair, peering out the window as he laid down the law of Bartertown to the trapper. "Skins of small animals," he said, eyeing the loaded cart, "we take ten percent. That's our cut . . . the rest is yours—trade it for what you want."

The trapper hesitated, frowning as he considered the percentage.

The Collector leaned further forward, lowering his voice. "Listen," he murmured, "the market's good. Four pelts will get you a sack of grain . . . or two hours with a woman." He raised his eyebrows.

The trapper brightened at the prospect. He spat into the palm of his hand. The Collector did the same. They shook hands, sealing the deal.

Four heavily armed men, three of them wearing gas masks, moved forward at the Collector's signal, began to search the cart and portion out the commission. They were Bartertown's Imperial Guards, their hair roached into a Mohawk cut, wearing rough uniforms of lizard skin and studded leather armor that left as much exposed as it covered—a testimony to their prowess or to the power of the desert's heat. Max studied them without seeming to, in particular the one without a mask, who wore an elaborate feathered headdress with a small skull set in its band like a jewel. He was a blunt bullet of a man; not as tall as the others but built like a tank. His heavily muscled torso and arms were decorated with elaborate tattooing. The Captain of the Bartertown Guard, he was called Ironbar Bassey. Anyone who had ever been unfortunate enough to cross him could swear to the appropriateness of his chosen name.

Max stepped up to the Collector's booth as the trapper moved on into the tunnel mouth.

The Collector looked him up and down, noting his gaunt, sunburned face and his lack of goods with obvious skepticism. "What are you trading?" he asked.

Max swallowed again, trying to force enough saliva down his raw throat to let words escape. "I'm looking for a man," he whispered.

"You got anything to trade or not?" the Collector interrupted.

"He was driving a camel train," Max went on, hoarsely, insistently. "He's got a weird laugh. . . ."

The Collector's pink, complacent face wrinkled like a hog's. He leaned forward again, gesturing at the sign out front with a fat hand; his arms were strung with half a dozen wristwatches each. "This is Barter-town—get it?" he said, his voice high and strident. "People come here to trade—do a little business, make a little profit. If you've got nothing to trade, you've got no business in Bartertown."

"One hour," Max said, "that's all I need."

The Collector looked past him at the next man in line, as if he had already ceased to exist. "Next." The trader behind Max pushed forward impatiently.

Max held his place stubbornly. "I've got skills—I can trade them," he said, desperation rasping in his voice. Rejection now meant a death sentence; he had no other choices left.

The Collector eyed him with smug amusement. "Sorry." He leered. "The brothel's full."

Max's hand shot out, seizing the Collector's leather tunic front and dragging him halfway out of the booth until the Collector's nearly hairless head and porcine face were inches from his own.

Ironbar Bassey and his men leaped forward, the Guard Captain swinging up a huge club studded with spikes.

Never taking his eyes off the Collector, Max reached under his robes with his free right hand, bringing up the sawed-off shotgun he wore slung at his side. He fired.

The blast shredded the feathers of Ironbar's headdress and stung his skull. The Guards skidded to a stop, feathers drifting down like snow around them. They stood frozen, along with everyone else within sight and hearing, all their eyes fixed on Max through the moment of excruciating silence that followed.

Max stood glaring back at them, the Collector's tunic-front still knotted in his fist, his shotgun pressed against the side of the man's head. He glanced at the Collector.

The Collector lifted his hand, signaling the Guards back.

"As I was saying," Max rasped, "one hour, that's all."

Sweating now, the Collector met his stare. "When you find him—what then?"

"I'll ask him to return what's mine," Max murmured.

"Of course." The Collector nodded agreeably, his eyes

white-ringed. "He's probably desperate to clear his conscience."

"Yeah." Max's eyes turned deadly. "He will be."

The Collector's gaze sharpened. His humoring banter fell away like a fatuous mask as he studied Max with sudden interest. "Oh, we think we're good, do we?" he asked.

Max nodded, unblinking. "Good enough."

The Collector glanced sidelong at Ironbar. The stranger was good enough to have put them both in a position they'd never been in before. . . . "Then he might have something to trade," he murmured. Ironbar nodded, answering some unspoken question.

"What's that?" Max asked, his grip on the Collector's collar tightening slightly.

The Collector looked back at him, bargaining seriously now. "Twenty-four hours of your time. In return you get back what's been stolen."

Max's face eased, barely, like his grip on the Collector's collar. "Sounds like a bargain."

"It's not," the Collector said. He gestured with a jerk of his head. "Let's talk. Inside . . ."

Max met his gaze, taking the measure of his trustworthiness, considering. . . . His hand loosened; the gun swung away from the Collector's head. The Collector jerked back and disappeared into his booth.

The Guards moved in the same instant, lunging forward. Max's gun swung up again in reflex, almost jamming itself up Ironbar Bassey's nose.

"Leave him!" The Collector appeared from a side passageway, gesturing frantically. Ironbar stepped back as the Collector joined Max, beckoning him on toward the waiting entrance to Bartertown. Max grimaced and lowered his gun again. Ironbar followed wordlessly, stalking down the tunnel with his club in his fist, like a heavily armed and badly singed turkey. His men followed without comment.

Midway through the shadowed tunnel they reached a kind of teller's window, a grilled opening to another room cut from the rock. The Collector stopped in front of the window. "Just one more thing . . ." He pointed to the crudely painted sign on the rock wall above the grill.

BARTERTOWN SUPPORTS
GUN CONTROL.
PARK YOUR WEAPONS HERE.

A gap-toothed man wearing a visor and a leather apron stepped into view behind the teller's window, smiling serenely. He was called Wristman, and he supervised weapons collection for all of Bartertown's guests.

Max looked up at the sign, down at Wristman, and shook his head.

"It's the law here," the Collector said flatly, moving closer to his side. The phalanx of Guards moved closer, too, surrounding him. "There are no exceptions."

Max hesitated a moment longer, feeling the pressure of half a dozen bodies ringing in his own, all of them armed with crossbows, knives, and clubs; the pressure of their combined wills against his mind . . . He slapped the shotgun down on the counter. Pulling open his robes, he unslung a crossbow and laid it down, unstrapped the dart gun from his forearm, unhooked the pouch of bullets from his belt. Wristman watched, still smiling, as he added his Geiger counter to the pile without comment. He pushed the pile under the grille and stepped back again.

The Collector inventoried the cache with a practiced eye. "No knife?" he said with smiling insinuation.

Max put his flyswatter between his teeth resignedly and leaned down to jerk a knife from inside his boot. Reaching over his shoulder, he pulled another knife from the sheath strapped at his back. Holding one knife in each fist, he threw them down; their blades dug into the teller's counter in front of him, quivered there side by side. Max shrugged, empty-handed, the flyswatter still clutched between his teeth.

Ironbar Bassey leaned forward, his hands sliding down Max's sides as he began a body search. Max stiffened like a wild animal; half turned, his hands knotting—

The Collector reached out, stopping the search as he saw Max's expression. "There's no need for that," he murmured. Max turned back to look at him, his muscles loosening. "Is there?" the Collector said meaningfully. He started on into the tunnel. Max took a deep breath and followed, and the Guards followed him in turn.

As they began to walk on into the tunnel, Wristman slid out of his cubbyhole. Pacing the Collector, he listened intently as the fat man murmured something in his ear. He nodded once, scuttled on ahead and disappeared into the brightening glow at the tunnel's mouth.

Max, armed only with his flyswatter, entered Bartertown.

The shock of what lay waiting for him made him blink, as full daylight and the town assailed his dazzled senses together. His face stayed expressionless with long years of habit, but his eyes widened as he took in the jumble of huts and tents, shanties and caves, pens and stalls, that covered the rocky terraces of the vast, abandoned mine pit. Strung together by a network of ladders and paths, the teeming junkyard village cascaded down to the floor of the open pit, circumscribing a central square reserved for commerce. Far more human beings than he could begin to count swarmed through the streets. Everywhere huge, blackened pipes pushed up out of the earth, belching smoke, steam, or flames like the chimneys of hell.

In the crowded square, which stretched on farther than his eyes could see, blacksmiths and wheelwrights hammered away at their trades, beating yesterday's wreckage into tomorrow's tools, adding their clanging to the shouts of merchants touting wares and the bellowing of livestock. Everywhere traders bartered, the way he should have been bartering—chickens for grain, grain for alcohol, alcohol for sex. A thousand different stenches multiplied and magnified into a miasma that stunned senses used to the aceticism of the desert. It was a shantytown, a drab, mud-colored, medieval ruin sprouting from the corpse of a civilization that refused to lie down and die . . . but it pulsed with new life and stubborn vitality, the closest thing to the world Before that Max had seen in almost twenty years.

Rising up in the center of town, dominating everything else, was a tall tower. Perched precariously at its tip, with a panoramic three-hundred-sixty-degree view of the squalor below, was the wasteland's only penthouse. Max stared at it, wondering vaguely who lived up there. Whoever it was must live like a lord—a king.

Directly before him now at the entrance was another signpost, its ragged slats of wood pointing in all directions, guiding new arrivals toward the various services and delights that Bartertown had to offer:

SMALL ANIMALS/FURS/COATS

BLACKSMITH/BROKEN LIMBS FIXED/SAWED OFF

PARADISE ALLEY

GARDENS OF PLEASURE/ANYTHING YOUR HEART DESIRES

FOOLS' WAY

Max wondered bleakly if he had already chosen the last. Above the signpost two of the Imperial Guards manned a watchtower, observing everyone who entered or left town. As Max looked up at them, his view was blocked by a bizarre apparition shambling past at the same height as the guard tower. A scrawny figure wearing sieve-sided goggles and a flying-saucer helmet topped by a light bulb drifted past with the ungainly gait of a giraffe. The bulb on the gawky giant's helmet shone like the light of inspiration, plugged into a battery pack on his back. The living cartoon strode away down a side street, following the string of naked light bulbs that festooned it like holiday decorations. As Max watched, the Bulbman checked light after light, replacing the burned-out bulbs with new ones. He walked on stilts, Max noticed at last, with a small start of relief. Bulbman disappeared into the maze of buildings as Max's escort herded him down one of the alleys toward his own uncertain destination.

Max followed the Collector silently, his restless gaze never lingering anywhere long as they made their way through one mobbed alley after another; trying to see as much, learn as much as he could about the unknown quantity that was Bartertown. Knowledge was survival. And somewhere in this Byzantine maze were his stolen goods and the son of a bitch who had stolen them.

He passed claustrophobic side alleys jammed with more stalls piled high with every imaginable kind of salvage, repair shops where things he had not realized even still existed were hacked apart and welded together and forced to live again. He watched a dentist, dressed appropriately in a slaughterman's bloodstained apron, drilling the teeth of a yowling patient perched on a barrel; the dentist also did blacksmithing, according to the sign over his head.

The screeches, yowls, and caterwauling of an open-air market in birds and small animals assailed him next; he glanced toward it, but he didn't see a monkey anywhere among the cages. The shouts and howls and whistles of the crowd in front of the Palace of Delight were hardly more civilized, as traders and locals ogled a live stage show where naked and nearly naked gyrating bodies lured the leering with promises of more and better inside.

Beyond the brothel they came out into a large open space where a man stood on a platform above the crowd, wearing a battered top hat and a tuxedo draping his bare chest. He was known as Dr. Dealgood—Bartertown's highly respected chief auctioneer and most flamboyant showman. He was flanked by two extremely good-looking women in minuscule fringed bikinis, who held up signs that read TODAY'S SPECIAL and wriggled suggestively to hold the crowd's attention. Glancing at their vapid, smirking faces, Max immediately dubbed them Tweedledum and Tweedledummer. He looked away again, unimpressed.

"It's an incredible beast," Dr. Dealgood was shouting, "the only off-road vehicle that'll never let you down." He gestured toward the pens beside him, flinging out his arms. "Desert, dunes, saltbush. You name it, the camel tames it. . . ."

Camels? Max stopped dead, looked back again with sudden interest. He raised his head, trying to see over the crowd. "Remember," Dr. Dealgood shouted, "this is the vehicle that sent Detroit broke—eight hundred miles to the gallon."

Max pushed forward through the crowd, the Collector and Ironbar Bassey following close behind him. Traders snarled as Max elbowed his way between them; their anger turned to fear as they saw who followed him. The

crowd melted aside, clearing his path toward the display
of livestock milling restlessly on the platform. Eight camels . . . his own camels, about to be sold out from under
him.

Dr. Dealgood glanced down as Max forced his way up
to the camels, noticing his unusual interest. This looked
like a real live one. . . . "They've got independent suspen-
sion, power steering—" One of the camels hiked its tail
sideways, and a pile of dung dropped to the ground
between its feet. Dr. Dealgood wrinkled his nose. "And
no emission control." He grinned, raising his eyebrows at
Max. "Once in a lifetime a unit like this comes on the
market. . . ."

Max reached up to fondle the snout of the nearest
camel; it lipped at his hand, responding with a fatuous,
rubbery smile to his familiar scent. "Where'd you get
'em?" he asked.

"A traveler." Dr. Dealgood shrugged. "Only traded
'em yesterday."

Max's eyes flickered away over the crowd and back.
"This traveler, he laughed funny?" He mimicked the
thief's demented laugh as closely as he could manage.

Dr. Dealgood nodded. "Yeah. That's him." He mimicked the laugh himself, perfectly, and the crowd
answered with laughter of its own.

A hand fell heavily on Max's shoulder as he opened his
mouth again; Ironbar Bassey jerked him backward.

"Those are my camels!" Max's hand shot out toward
the platform in protest, laying claim.

"Those were your camels," Bassey snarled. "C'mon."
His hand closed painfully, pressing a nerve. Max winced
and let himself be led on his way, as behind him Dr.
Dealgood shrugged off his bad luck and began his spiel to

the crowd once more. "Ride 'em away now. . . . Make me an offer!"

"A stallion and three Indians!" the bounty hunter with the Hare Krishnas shouted.

"I'll take the horse." Dr. Dealgood motioned him forward. "You can keep the gurus."

Max walked on, his fists clenched, not looking back.

CHAPTER 3

ENTITY

Max and his escort reached their destination at last: the concrete-shod base of the steel- and wood-frame tower he had seen before, the one with the penthouse at its top. Looking up into the knotted and welded tangle of the tower's framework, Max realized that he was probably about to find out who lived up there after all. He wondered whether he would be glad or sorry when he knew.

Wristman, the weapons-checker, stood waiting for them beside a crude wooden cage that appeared to be Bartertown's version of an elevator. It reminded Max of a bird cage, built large enough to hold three or four humans captive, suspended from a system of pulleys and cables. The Collector stepped in through its doorway without hesitation; Max followed with Ironbar treading on his heels.

Wristman secured the flimsy door and gave a signal.

Creaking and swaying, the elevator began to rise from the ground. Max hung on to the grid beside him, looking up at the wooden platform they were rising toward, out and down again as more and more of Bartertown was displayed in festering panorama below him. He tried to retrace the path that had brought him here through the maze of its streets; couldn't. All at once his view was cut off as the elevator rose through the penthouse floor.

The basket jerked gently to a halt. Max turned, seeing two more Imperial Guards, one of them with his hand still on the lever that controlled the elevator.

The Collector pushed open the door and stepped out. Max followed, staring around him silently, feeling as if he had stepped into a dream. It was beautiful; he had not seen anything beautiful in longer than he could remember. The space around him was suffused with a luminous glow; it was like walking into a room of light. Where a solid roof and walls should have been, there was nothing but fine muslin, billowing softly in the breeze, seeming to breathe and shift like a living thing. The gossamer cloth was spotlessly, pristinely white. Music drifted to them on the warm air, adding to the unreality of the moment— the haunting, plaintive sound of a saxophone. Even as he wondered fleetingly about his sanity, Max thought that whoever was playing the sax was very, very good.

The Collector started on across the room without comment. Ironbar Bassey gave Max an ungentle shove, forcing him to follow. They passed through a curtain of gauze into another, larger space beyond.

The room beyond the curtain had an almost Oriental simplicity, as if it has been designed to bring the mind to peaceful meditation and the eye to rest. A long, low table holding a pewter pitcher and a silver platter of fruit was its centerpiece; a hammock chair of skillfully knotted silk rope hung motionless on the far side of the room. The startling green of potted plants stood out along the walls, and a ceiling fan hummed faintly overhead, stirring and cooling the air. The saxophone player sat near the table, cross-legged on a pallet, wearing only a loincloth and a few beaded ornaments. He was black and middle-aged, with a mostly shaven head and a stocky torso. The skin of his forehead and chest and had been artfully scarred in elaborate swirling patterns. His name was Tonton Tattoo.

His fingers moved fluidly over the keys of his instrument; he seemed totally lost in his music. Max stared at him, unable to believe that someone could so completely ignore their intrustion . . . until he looked into the man's eyes, which were as dim and dead as stones. The man was blind.

"Rachmaninoff," a woman's voice, deep and vibrant, said.

Max looked up again, startled, as a pair of slender, long-fingered hands parted another curtain of gauze on the far side of the room. A woman stepped through. Not any woman. Aunty Entity. She was not young—he guessed that she was at least his own age—but her body was firm and taut beneath a calf-length dress of silver metal mesh that left almost nothing to his imagination. Her hair was silver-blond, worn in a hawk's-crest cascade, her skin the color of coffee with cream. She wore masses of bracelets and heavy earrings . . . and, incredibly, high-heeled shoes. "You remember Rachmaninoff?" she said softly.

Max did not answer. Her body was worth looking at, but it was her face that his eyes stayed on: the strong, sensuous features; the measuring intelligence in her eyes; the confidence, the sheer, riveting magnetism of her gaze that went through him like electricity.

The Collector moved to Max's side. "He's a warrior, Aunty . . . looking for a deal." His hand flicked out at Max's chest. Max realized suddenly that this woman was the owner of the penthouse . . . the ruler of Bartertown. *A woman.* You didn't see many women with that kind of power these days. And yet, looking at her, somehow he was not at all surprised.

The woman looked Max up and down in turn, her glance raking his torn, filthy clothing, his wild hair and haggard face. She folded her arms, looking away at Ironbar, at the shredded remains of his Captain's head-dress. "And he beat you?" Bassey looked down at his feet, his naked scalp reddening.

"You're going soft, Ironbar," she murmured with a trace of sarcasm, a drop of venom. She bent her head at Max. "Look at him, he's just a raggedy man." Her voice was smooth and biting, like fine whiskey.

Ironbar glanced up, stung. "He's quick," he protested.

Aunty Entity moved forward toward Max; her every movement had the sinuous grace of a stalking cat. She reached out, gently removing the flyswatter from his hand. His hands tightened and flexed as she circled him, assessing, tapping the flyswatter on her open palm. "You think he can do it?" She turned back to Ironbar.

Ironbar hesitated, caught under her gaze like a bug. "I dunnno," he muttered, "maybe . . . " He glanced at the stranger, a look full of snakes.

She turned back to Max, standing face-to-face with him for the first time. "What did you do?" she asked. "Before this?"

Somehow he knew she did not simply mean before Bartertown. "I was a cop," he muttered hoarsely, "a driver." The words, the identity, seemed almost meaningless to him now.

But Entity raised her eyebrows. "A Bronze?" she said. "Oh, you were good!" Her voice mocked him, but her eyes studied him with a new respect. Stretching her arm, she pushed the flyswatter under the hems of his loose robes and began to lift them casually, like someone inspecting a horse. "How the world turns..." she murmured, musing, amused. She eyed his stained and threadbare trousers, the rusty metal brace that he had fitted for his bad knee. "One day cock of the walk"— she hiked the robes to his waist, her eyes following them brazenly up to his belt buckle: regulation police issue, the letters MFP emblazoned in indestructable brass—"next, a feather duster." Her mouth quirked.

She let his robes fall and tossed him the flyswatter. He caught it easily, almost too quickly, as she turned away. "Play something, Tonton," she said, "something tragic."

The musician had stopped playing, sat waiting silently as she had entered the room. Now he lifted his instrument unerringly to his lips and began to play again, a mournful thread of melody.

Entity turned back to Max, a curious smile still pulling at the edges of her lips. The smile faded. "You know who I was?" she said. "Nobody. But on the day after I was still alive." She leaned over, picked a fresh apple from the shining platter on the table, weighing it in her palm like Justice. "This nobody had the chance to be somebody." She held his gaze for a long moment, and he saw more emotions pass over her face in that one moment than he could have named in a lifetime.

She turned away from him abruptly, snapping the wire of tension between them. "So much for history." She waved a desultory hand at the table. "Anyway, help yourself. Water, fruit..."

Behind him Max sensed a faint, shifting movement

among the Guards. He hesitated, his eyes on the woman's expressionless face; looked down after a moment, studying the fruit, his hand hovering above it. Watching him, Entity bit into her apple. The sudden, juicy crunch of fresh fruit filled the room, not quite disguising another far more familiar sound.

In one motion Max wiped everything from the tray, grabbed it by the rim; turned and hurled the tray like a discus. The tray caught Ironbar Bassey straight in the throat and knocked him sprawling backward. The machete he had drawn as Entity bit into the apple flew from his hand as he crashed to the floor, the plate wedged into his neck.

As Max struck, another Guard raised his arm, aiming his wrist crossbow, and fired. Max caught the movement from the corner of his eye, ducked just as the arrow whizzed past his head. The bolt struck Tonton Tattoo's saxophone; it wailed like a mortally wounded sheep. Tonton jerked in surprise, dropping the instrument with a cry.

Max lunged forward, grabbing the Guard by the arm, yanking him off-balance and heaving him over his back. The Guard came down on one end of the long, low table, flipping it. Its far end smashed up into the second Guard's face like a rising seesaw as he ran forward, throwing him back again and through one of the curtained walls of the penthouse. The fragile cloth ripped like tissue, and Max heard his scream as he fell three stories into the street below.

The Guard landed with a backbreaking crash on the raised end of an acrobat's teeterboard down below, catapulting the woman balanced on its other end high into the air. She soared across the street, directly into the arms of the passing Bulbman. His stilts flew out from under him with the unexpected impact; he grabbed at the light cable desperately as he began to fall. The cable snapped, dumping him and the woman backward into a tent full of foods and squawking chickens. The broken power cable snapped and thrashed like a snake having a seizure; passers by yelled and ran.

The sounds of chaos below carried clearly into the penthouse, but Max's mind was on more pressing business. He started forward as Ironbar struggled up from the floor, clutching his ruined throat; ready to kick the Guard's face in. A movement came at him from the side; he spun back as the Collector charged in from his right, swinging a double-bladed ax. Max threw himself backward, dodging the blow that would have sheared off an arm; the ax head buried itself in the floor between his boots.

The Collector heaved furiously on the ax's handle, looking up at Max as he tried to wrench it free. Max looked back at him for an instant that seemed to last an eternity. And then he stepped forward, kicking the ax handle upward. The handle smashed into the Collector's groin with a resounding thwack. The Collector staggered backward, his eyes bulging, his mouth open in a silent howl of agony. Max caught up a piece of fruit and jammed it into his gaping mouth.

Max backed away again, breathing hard as he began to turn, his eyes searching the room. A rope dropped down over his head; behind him, Ironbar Bassey yanked the noose tight around his neck, twisting it at the end of a heavy pole.

Max's hands flew to his throat, clawing at the rope as the noose crushed his windpipe, cutting off his air. The more he struggled, the more it tightened. His head sang, his lungs screamed; Ironbar's taunting grin, Entity's cool impassive gaze swam blood-red in front of his eyes, never leaving his face ... Desperately he fumbled for the flyswatter dangling from his wrist, grabbed its handle, and jerked it apart. Light shone on metal as he pulled a long blade from the hollow handle.

He reached up blindly and slashed the noose apart. Sucking in a ragged gasp of air, he caught the pole in both hands, wrenching hard and twisting. Its other end was knotted firmly around Bassey's wrist. Max drove forward and jerked the pole up, forcing Ironbar's arm with it. Bassey reeled backward as his own fist punched him in the mouth. Max jerked the pole upward again and again, driving Ironbar's fist into his face over and over until he sprawled forward, unconscious, onto the carpet.

The click of a weapon being cocked behind him echoed in the sudden silence.

Max turned slowly. Entity still watched him impassively from across the room. But now she held a small, high-powered crossbow in her hands, pointed squarely at his heart. Max's clenched hands loosened; he stood motionless, his breath rasping, his body twitching with exhaustion.

Behind him the Collector rose painfully from the floor. He hobbled past Max to Entity's side. "I said he was good ... " he wheezed.

Max glanced at him and grimaced. "No," he said hoarsely, "just lucky."

Two Guards burst through the curtains from the elevator, answering the commotion they had heard up above. They headed for Max, weapons drawn.

Entity lifted her hand, signaling them to stop. She lowered her own crossbow. "Congratulations," she said. "You're the first to survive the audition." She glanced around her ruined sitting room, leaned down to pick up the half-empty water pitcher lying on the floor beside the upended table. She offered it to him silently.

Max's cracked lips tightened. Frowning, he shook his head.

"It's all right," she said, almost surprised. "It's fine. . . . "

Max's hands stayed motionless at his sides.

Entity raised the pitcher to her own lips, sipped a mouthful, gargled it, and swallowed.

Max lunged forward, jerking the pitcher from her hands. He gulped water until the pitcher was empty, the clear, cold liquid splashing down over his chin and chest, putting out the fire in his throat. He set the pitcher down. Catching up a piece of the scattered fruit, he began to choke it down in huge bites. He had not seen fruit like this in two or three years; but what should have been a rare feast meant nothing more to his starving body than something to fill its empty, aching gut. Behind him, he heard Ironbar and the other Guard recovering consciousness, stumbling to their feet. He picked up another piece of fruit and went on eating unconcernedly, oblivious to the silent stares of everyone around him.

Entity stood waiting until Max had blunted his thirst and hunger and then gestured for him to join her. He crossed the room to stand beside her as she drew back the curtain of gauze, bringing Bartertown into view below. "Look around, mister," she said, gazing out over the bustling surge of life below them. Max glanced at the view, went back to his eating; his hunger had dulled enough now that he was beginning to be able to enjoy what he ate. The sweet, succulant feel of pith and juice sliding down his throat was almost an erotic pleasure.

"All of this I built," Entity said, the pride of her voice forcing its way into his attention. "Up to my armpits in blood and shit, but where there was desert, there's a town; where there was robbery, there's trade; where there was despair, there's hope . . . ." She turned away from the view, turning toward him again, forcing him to look at her. He met her gaze wordlessly, still eating.

"I'll do anything to protect it," she said, and he believed her. "Now it's necessary to kill a man." Her eyes narrowed. "Interested?"

Max paused, the orange halfway to his lips. He took another bite. "What do you pay?" he asked, his face expressionless.

"I'll re-equip you, your vehicle—animals, whatever." She watched him for a reaction. "Fuel, if you want it," offering him the one thing worth more than gold.

Max said nothing.

"It's a generous offer." She shifted restlessly, settling her hands on her hips.

"Why me?" Max said at last. "You've got weapons, warriors, just give the order ."

"Listen to him, Aunty," Ironbar grated, holding his throat. "We never got nothing by mincing around."

Entity did not acknowledge him, still studying Max with dark, thoughtful eyes. "I'm dealing with subtleties here," she said. "This is no enemy—it's almost family ." He almost thought he heard regret. She glanced away for the first time, gazing out the window.

Max's mouth twitched. "Real civilized," he said, unimpressed.

A faint frown furrowed her smooth forehead. She looked back at him again. "The reasons don't concern you"— her voice sharpened, reminding him of who and where he was—"just the conditions. You wanna deal or not?"

Max nodded, having already considered the alternatives.

Her face showed him nothing now, however she felt about his decision. "First," she said, leaning hard on each word, "nobody knows you work for me. You hit him and you go. Second, it's a fair fight. Third—it's to the death."

Max nodded again. It sounded more honest than he'd expected. Maybe she meant what she said after all. Not that it mattered. "Who's the bunny?"

Entity turned away from the window, led him back across the penthouse to the far side of the littered living room. They stopped before the place where a vaguely familiar-looking length of pipe rose up through the floor; Max realized that it was some kind of periscope. Its range extended far below the penthouse, below the base of the tower itself, deep into the bowels of the abandonded mines below. Using a primitive but ingeniously designed system of lights and mirrors, it allowed Entity a perfectly safe view of the vast cavern system that was Bartertown's hidden underground. Ironbar drew the viewing slot down from the ceiling to eye level; the Collector pushed forward a chair as Entity took hold of the periscope's crosspiece and sat down.

Entity beckoned Max to her side, offering him a share of the viewing slot as she began to peer through it. Max sat uncertainly on a corner of the chair, his shoulder brushing hers, their faces almost touching. His reviving senses began to register the contact of his flesh and hers, the scent and sight and closeness of a beautiful woman. He glanced at her; her eyes ignored him, but her body didn't. She knew what she was doing. He wished he knew why. With an effort he shifted his concentration back to the scope, tried to orient his eyes to the murky darkness that was all he could see. A confusion of bizarre images flickered past as the periscope lowered and swung in a random arc across a subterranean world that he had never even imagined existed beneath the one he stood in now.

The lens tracked along a tangled snarl of ceiling pipes, through clouds of steam, came to rest on the first thing he could clearly recognize. Among the infernal forest of boilers, pipes, and heavy wooden beams, a sign hung from a chain. It read, ATTILA THE HEN IS WATCHING YOU. Without moving his head Max glanced at the woman beside him again. Her own face was expressionless as she guided the periscope's lens past the sign raised like a defiant finger by someone down below. There were always two sides to a story . . . at least two.

Max's eyes widened as he looked back through the viewing slot. Beyond the sign the cavern opened out into a vast, brooding maze of pipes and machinery, dimly lit by arc lights and distant shafts of sunlight filtering down through massive overhead ventilation grates. He realized that all this must underlie the marketplace he had passed through on his way to the penthouse. The centerpiece of the complex was an ancient locomotive engine, still sitting on tracks, which must once have hauled ore up out of the bowels of the mine. Now it had mutated into a sedentary power plant, its rusted-out hulk rebuilt with parts of an old truck body and imprisoned forever underground, shackled to a bewildering array of pipes and gauges.

But the marvels of post-holocaust engineering were not the thing that Max's eyes found the most difficult to believe. It was the presence, everywhere he looked, of countless thousands of pigs. Their pens and enclosures spread away into the shadowed distance for as far as his eyes could see, rank on rank of them, all grunting, foraging, and crapping as if there were nothing at all extraordinary about their presence there. Their quarters were sumptuous by animal standards—or even human standards these days—well supplied with brimming troughs of food and water. Countless human tenders moved among them, hosing them down, scrubbing them off, shoveling their dung into wheelbarrows. In the foreground of the scope's view several workers clustered together, massaging a huge old sow, for reasons Max could not even guess at. It seemed to him that he could almost hear the sounds of grunting and heavy machinery echoing through the caverns down below, almost smell the appalling reek. . . . He realized suddenly that vision was not the only thing the periscope's pipe supplied.

"It's called the Underworld," Entity said. "It's where Bartertown gets its energy."

Max tore his gaze from the incredible sight before him to look back at her. "What," he asked, "oil, natural gas?"

She shook her head, her earrings batting softly against her throat. "Pigs."

Max glanced at the scope again and pointed. "You mean—pigs? Like those?"

Entity nodded. "That's right."

Max's mouth pulled down. "Bullshit."

She met his sardonic stare, held it, her own gaze unyielding, until he believed that she was perfectly serious. "Pigshit," she said.

"What?" Max looked at her blankly.

"The lights, donkey motors—our vehicles—they all use a high-powered gas." She smiled, an amused teacher instructing a difficult pupil. "It's called methane. And you make methane from pigshit." Lifting her hand, she caught his chin gently, almost caressingly, with her cupped fingers. She drew his face back toward the eye-piece, adjusting its sight with her free hand. Side by side they peered through the viewing slot again.

This time Max's view of the Underworld showed him a group of men, their own faces vaguely piglike behind the muzzles and goggles of gas masks. They were emptying semi-liquid excrement out of something that looked like a mine car by shovelfuls and bucketfuls. The lens panned back toward the mutant locomotive, searching until it found a raised wooden platform snarled with pipes, on which the large corrugated tank of a boiler sat, sur-rounded by more dials and gauges. On the far side of the platform he saw what appeared to be two workers being dressed down by a much smaller man wearing goggles and what looked like a samurai helmet. The man doing the yelling was not only small but also old, and Max was surprised at the fear he saw on the workers' faces.

And then the small man began to raise, higher and higher, as the two technicians stepped back, looking up. The small man was only the size of a child, and he was riding a saddle . . . perched like a shriveled bird on the back of a rhino, on the shoulders of the most enormous and powerful-looking man that Max had ever seen. The big man's face and head were entirely hidden inside an elaborately segmented metal helmet. The effect was not simply bizarre but monstrous, like the carapace of some highly magnified insect. But this was real. The two work-ers backed away with obsequious haste. As Max watched, the small man leaned forward, speaking direc-tions into an ear horn built into the big man's helmet. Secure on the giant's shoulders, he leaned back again smugly, taking a drag from a long cheroot.

The grotesque parasitic pair began to climb the steps of the wooden platform, which Max now saw had been built around the captive locomotive. They crossed the shadowed platform, one being in every meaningful way. The giant stopped at the near edge of the platform, clutching the rail with a ham-sized, gauntleted hand as his small, wizened partner surveyed their domain with a self-satisfied smile.

They hovered dead-center in the frame of the viewing slot as Entity's hand trained the periscope directly on them.

"Who's that?" Max asked, already guessing why his attention was being focused on them. *So this was his target . . . .*

"MasterBlaster," Entity said. "He's the man who makes it work. He runs Underworld."

Max looked back at her. "Which one?" he asked, surprised at the strength of his own curiosity.

"They're a unit." She nodded at the scope. "They even share the name. The little one's the brain—he's called Master. The other one's the muscle—he's Blaster." Max looked through the lens again. "Together they're very powerful."

That sounded like an understatement. As Max watched, the tiny man—Master—glanced up, his face freezing into an expression that could only be hatred as he looked Max straight in the eye. Max pulled back, until it struck him that all Master could have seen was the lowered periscope keeping him under observation. Master shouted something into Blaster's ear, and Blaster began to stride on along the platform. As they passed two workers pushing a large trolley filled with brown liquid, Master spoke into the ear horn again. Blaster leaned out obediently, catching up a dripping gob of what looked like mud but wasn't. Turning back toward the lens as Master pointed, he threw it hard.

Max and Entity jerked back involuntarily as the pig-shit splatted home in a perfect bull's-eye on the lens. Rising up the shaft from down below, they heard Master's high-pitched, crazy laughter.

"They're also arrogant," Entity murmured dryly. She closed the viewing slot, the movement abrupt with barely controlled anger. "I want to keep the brain. Dump the body." She stood up, looking down at him. "Are you good enough? Can you kill Blaster?"

Max rose from his seat, looking back at her for a long moment before he answered. 'He's big. How good is he?"

Entity raised the periscope. "He can beat most men with his breath." Ironbar and Collector flanked her like statutes, their hands resting on their hips as they waited for his response.

"I wanna see him close," Max said at last. "How do I get in there?"

Entity shrugged an elaborately draped shoulder. "It's a factory. Ask for work." The smoldering heat had disappered from her gaze when she looked at him. Now he understood: Only victors were rewarded. She turned away, pushing between Ironbar and the Collector as if Max had disappeared too.

Max shook his head, half frowning. "I don't know anything about methane."

Entity turned back abruptly, her eyes like flint. "You can shovel shit, can't you?" She turned away again, stepped through the billowing white curtains, and was gone.

CHAPTER 4

UNDERWORLD

Max shoveled shit. Getting the job had been easy . . . the shit patrol didn't get many applicants. The other three members of his work team were all convicts; dangling against their chests were tags identifying their crimes: THIEF, DEAL BUSTER, PIG KILLER. They wore metal collars around their necks, shackles on their wrists; heavy chains clanked bruisingly against their arms and sides every time they took a step or lifted a shovel.

Max lifted another shovelful of reeking manure and dumped it into a waiting cart that was nearly full already. His arms ached from the strain of unused muscles. He figured that he'd been here for three or four hours, and already he had come to believe that if he never saw another pig, it would be too soon. His own sense of smell had died a quick and unpleasant death within the first hour after his arrival in the Underworld, the only thing he could now think of to be grateful for. He had thrown away his loose, hanging robes, which were nothing but a magnet for filth in his present job; his ragged, black T-shirt was soaked with sweat and splattered with manure.

He straightened up, stretching the knotted muscles in his back, wiping more sweat from his eyes with a gloved hand. The heat was as bad down here as it was up in town, and the humidity was much higher. The air was as thick as soup. He glanced away into the gloom of the light-and-shadowed cavern with what he hoped looked like casual indifference. Around him scores of other men and women—convicts, slaves, and outcasts like himself—moved like the damned through the lowest circle of hell, working at various tasks, most of them pleasanter than his own. He spotted the three Hare Krishnas he had seen early this morning; still chained together, they were scrubbing down several large, inanely grinning porkers.

His collection crew was nearing the observation platform at last; they had been working their way toward it, shovelful by shovelful, all morning. Putting his shoulder to the cart along with one of the convicts, he pushed it another ten feet toward his goal. Straightening again, he took a deep, pungent breath. From here he could see the platform clearly at last. Master and Blaster were up there, facing away from him; he heard Master's cackling laughter, Blaster's eerie metallic echo of it. They seemed to be playing with something.

Max drifted away from the cart, carrying his shovel, trying for a better look at Blaster. All at once a small, furry, brown face popped up over Blaster's massive shoulder, meeting his stare across the crowd of swine and humans. Max started, seeing his own monkey in the hands of MasterBlaster. He took a step forward and then another, dragging the shovel behind him as he started toward the platform.

The monkey chattered in shrill delight and clapped its hands. It clambered lightly down Blaster's arm, starting toward the steps, toward Max. Max pushed forward unthinkingly through the sea of pigs, holding out his hand. Behind him, the nearest of the convicts stopped shoveling to stare in curiosity.

Abruptly Blaster's huge bulk turned and started after the monkey. MasterBlaster loomed above Max on the platform, even bigger than he had imagined, jerking on a leash attached to the monkey's collar—snapping the monkey up short, dragging it back up the stairs.

"Hey!" Max shouted angrily. "Leave him alone."

Blaster laughed, his laughter echoing weirdly inside his helmet, like something rising up from the bottom of a well. He tugged on the leash again, dragging the shrieking monkey back across the platform.

Max started forward again, fury burning in the pit of his stomach. He had thought this would be unpleasant, challenging Blaster, setting him up. . . . He had been wrong. It would be easy. And maybe it would happen a lot faster than anybody had expected.

A hand in a reeking leather glove fell on his shoulder, pulling him to a halt.

Max spun around, his eyes like glass; he found himself face-to-face with one of the convicts on his work team. It was Pig Killer, the one who had stood silently watching his progress toward doom. "C'mon, free man," Pig Killer said gently, with a good-natured grin that didn't touch the warning in his eyes. "Help a convict. . . ." His hand stayed on Max's shoulder, pulling him back toward the shit buckets with subtle but irresistible pressure. "You don't want to end up like me." He raised his eyebrows.

Max stared at Pig Killer for a long moment, at his filth-smeared face and the chains dangling against his chest. He glanced away again, taking in the vast, mobbed cavern, as claustrophobic as a prison . . . and as well guarded. Slowly the anger drained out of him, letting him think clearly again. He looked back at Pig Killer, really seeing him for the first time. Pig Killer was about his own height, probably in his late twenties, with close-cropped brown hair and brown eyes. His sweating, weary face wasn't one that Max would have expected to find smiling, at him or anybody else, under the circumstances. Max sighed and shrugged and followed Pig Killer back to the nearest barrel.

"How long you in for?" Max asked.

Pig Killer jerked a shoulder. "The big one. Life."

"For killing a pig?" Max said, incredulous. Who the hell would even miss one? But he knew exactly who would and exactly why.

"No"— Pig Killer's smile disappeared—"for trying to feed my family." His dark eyes flickered down. Max felt the twinge of a buried loss, choked the feeling off before his mind could even put a name to it.

Pig Killer looked back at him, the incongruous whimsy pulling his mouth up again. "But I'm not worried. Down here life's about two and a half years."

Max stared at him. He remembered, incongruously and completely unexpectedly, an ancient joke about an eternal optimist: a kid had been shut up in a room full of horse manure as an experiment. When the psychologists came back for him, he was digging happily through the ton of shit, saying, "There must be a pony in here somewhere." Max shook his head and put his shoulder to one side of the barrel full of excrement. Together they began to wrestle the slopping barrel through the sea of grunting

animals, around past the front of the imprisoned
locomotive.

Up on the platform Max heard the monkey whimper
as Blaster reeled it back to his side. He looked over his
shoulder, watching as Blaster picked the monkey up in a
huge fist, stroking its back. MasterBlaster turned, following Max's progress through the pigyard below. Master
frowned, feeling the heat of Max's sullen stare, meeting
it with his own, marking the face of the man who had
almost challenged his position. He studied Max a
moment longer, and then he signaled Blaster; with a final
warning look they turned and strode away.

Max released the breath he had been holding without
realizing it. They reached the cart and raised the barrel
of pig crap together, dumping it into the waiting lake of
brown sludge. "Ever wondered what happens in your
guts?" Pig Killer asked.

Max felt his clenched jaw surprise him by suddenly
trying to grin. He shook his head emphatically.

"You're looking at it," Pig Killer said, undeterred.
"One big chemical reaction." They set the bucket down
again and threw their joined weight against the rear of
the cart, starting it on along the track through the squealing carpet of hogs. "All that crap . . . fermenting . . . giving off a gas. That's what those pipes are for." He jerked
his head, pointing up at the platform with his chin. "They
take it to the boiler."

As they made their way past the side of the locomotive,
Max saw a tiny house farther along the platform, con-
structed from what had once been a gaudily painted
circus wagon; it rested now on a flatbed railroad car.
MasterBlaster's home. Its cheerful, luridly festive presence in a place like this was almost surreal. Max won-

dered if MasterBlaster ever went above ground. That would even the odds. . . .

They passed the three Hare Krishnas, working now at massaging another grinning sow, while Pig Killer rattled on about methane, not seeming to care whether Max was really listening or not. "In goes the gas, out comes the energy, on go the lights. It's not Exxon, but it works. That's the power of the little guy—his knowledge. . . ."

MasterBlaster emerged from behind the locomotive again as Pig Killer spoke, strolling along the gantry like some monster out of a Japanese movie, the God of Death. Max's gaze followed Blaster's every movement, looking for some sign of weakness; his face hardened over again.

"You may not like the man," Pig Killer said, raising his voice as he saw Max's muscles tense, "but you gotta admire the mind. . . ."

Max glanced back at him absently. "Yeah," he murmured, forcing himself to sound interested. "But how much gas can you get?" He looked away again, as a mechanic in a baseball cap approached MasterBlaster, gesturing, talking animatedly. Their conversation was completely lost in the echoing choir of grunting and squealing around him. MasterBlaster began to follow the mechanic away down the catwalk, heading toward another chamber.

"Depends on the food," Pig Killer said, relieved, not noticing that Max's attention had already wandered again. "Pigs are like humans. Works best with beans." He laughed, looking back at Max for a reaction.

Max was gone.

Pig Killer stopped pushing the cart, glancing away around the cavern in surprise and confusion. In the distance Max was disappearing down a tunnel, following MasterBlaster toward another chamber. Pig Killer shook

his head and began to push the cart on down the line
alone.

Max emerged from the tunnel into a part of the
Underworld he had not seen before. The chamber had
been turned into a garage; rows of dune buggies, off-road
vehicles, and bizarre-looking dirt bikes sat parked along
the walls. All of them had undergone radical structural
modifications, from previous repairs with makeshift
parts, or to armor and reinforce their bodies; most of
them seemed to be undergoing more repair work now. All
of them sprouted gas cylinders instead of fuel tanks,
converted to run on methane.

In the center of the workshop a group of technicians
and workers had gathered, with MasterBlaster standing
among them, towering over them. They stood around an
off-road vehicle as bizarre and battered as the rest but
somehow oddly familiar. As Max came up behind them,
he realized with a sudden pang of recognition that it was
his own dune buggy. A pair of boots protruded from
underneath it, like the feet of a corpse sticking out of a
mortuary drawer.

Max stopped, standing in the shadows at the edge of
the workshop, watching and listening. Blaster's foot
tapped a protruding boot; Blackfinger, Entity's head
mechanic, slid out from beneath the vehicle, his face
furrowed with worry.

"Edsel's right," the mechanic said. He gestured at the
car above him with a filthy hand. "We've got a problem.
At least twelve pounds of gelignite."

Master frowned and shrugged impatiently. "Problem?
You expert. Disarm." Max was surprised, not for the first
time today, to hear the mastermind of Underworld talking like a three-year-old. Blaster's foot kicked Black-

finger's trolly back under the dune buggy and the mechanic with it.

"Knackered if I know how it's rigged." Blackfinger's voice drifted up through the car's exposed entrails as he studied the clumped dynamite sticks wired to its undercarriage. "It's a class job." He emerged again, this time cautiously on the far side of the vehicle. "One mistake, it'll blow the crap out of this place. Literally."

Master's frown deepened. "What to do?" he cried irritably. "Leave here? Cost good trade. Me drive." He struck his chest with his hand.

The mechanic walked around the front of the car, studying the problem from a fresh angle. He ran a grease-stained hand through his black, curly hair. "I could disconnect the battery."

"I wouldn't do that." Max stepped out of the shadows as they turned, staring. He started forward, letting them see his face clearly. "The clamps are on detonators."

Master craned his neck from behind Blaster's shoulder, peering at Max like an indignant parrot perched in a tree. Blaster started forward at his signal. "Who you?" he demanded.

"Me Max." Max kept walking, his mouth twisting sardonically, until Blaster was an arm's length in front of him. There was only one way he could get close enough to MasterBlaster to know what he was really up against. . . . He stopped; the mechanics peered past MasterBlaster, watching him with bug-eyed fascination. His own head barely came up to Blaster's shoulder; the giant weighed probably half again as much as he did.

Master glowered. "You smart," he said, his voice whining with malice. "Dead quick."

Max pointed. "That's my vehicle."

Master's face did not change. "You live. Disarm."

"How much?" Max put his hands on his hips.

"No trade," Master brayed. "Do!"

Max shook his head and started to turn away.

Master leaned over the ear horn, giving Blaster another order. "Fetch!"

Blaster moved forward like a tank, reaching Max in one stride, catching him by the scruff of the neck. Max turned back, instinctively struggling, but it was already too late. Blaster's other hand closed around his throat. Blaster lifted him completely off the ground, as if he were no heavier than Master. Max's hands rose, prying at the steel-sinewed fingers clutching his throat; his flailing legs lashed out viciously, searching for purchase or a vulnerable spot. But Blaster only tightened his grip, as unconcerned as if his body were made of stone, and choked his captive into submission.

Max stopped struggling, realizing quickly enough the futility of his resistance as Blaster held him up at eye level with the frowning Master. "Me order," the tiny, shriveled face hissed. "Me Master. Run Bartertown."

"Sure." Max gasped. "That's why you live in shit."

"Not shit," Master said coldly, "energy."

Max's mouth thinned. "Call it what you like. It still smells like shit."

"Energy!" Master shouted. Blaster gave his captive a shake, like a mastiff shaking a rat. "No energy, no town. Me king Arab." Master struck himself on the chest again.

"Oh, sure," Max said through gritted teeth. "Me fairy princess."

Master's face turned a mottled red with disbelief and fury. "Embargo. On!" he shouted into Blaster's ear horn. Blaster lowered Max until his feet touched the floor again. Keeping a viselike grip on Max's shirt, Blaster began to stride out of the workshop, dragging their prisoner behind him.

MasterBlaster hauled Max ignominiously up the steps, onto the catwalk surrounding the locomotive, and herded him back toward the main control panel that routed electricity to every part of Bartertown. Max saw a confusion of gauges, levers, and switches, and what looked like an ancient steering wheel. Master flicked a switch querulously, watched while Blaster slowly and with obvious effort began to turn the wheel.

And in the town above, things began to happen . . . or stop happening. The clamor of frantic bartering and trading suddenly died as traders and merchants alike looked up in alarm. Jedediah, dickering over a salvaged propeller blade as he traded off the last of Max's possessions, looked up with the rest as the constant background throb of machine noise began to falter and die somewhere down below his feet. Silence fell across the entire city as the motley inhabitants of Bartertown stared at one another in sudden dread. In the central square Dr. Dealgood's blaring microphone suddenly cut off, accentuating the deathly quiet.

At the entrance gate new arrivals stood patiently in line as the Collector passed judgment on them, one by one. Ironbar Bassey looked on from his station inside the tunnel entrance, his neck wrapped in bandages, as traders surrendered their ten percent. He looked up in surprise, along with everyone else, as the industrial lights strung overhead in the tunnel flickered once and blacked out. He glanced at the Collector with a look of knowing disgust.

In Entity's penthouse Tonton Tattoo sat playing a peaceful melody on his saxophone. Lying back in her white mesh hammock, Entity swayed in gentle rhythm to the music, content for the first time in months, soothed by the thought that fate had sent her the tool she had needed at last ... that ragged, brooding stranger, the unlikeliest champion she or Bartertown would ever have. But when she had looked into his eyes ...

The ceiling fan above her head faltered and slowed. Entity's eyes snapped open as it sighed to a stop, and she heard ... nothing. She pushed herself up from the hammock, her face hard with outrage.

Back in the Underworld Master sniggered with satisfaction. All that told Max it was laughter was the grin on Master's face. Never taking his eyes off Max, Master began to count down: "Four ... three ... two ..." His diminutive hand shot out, pointing at a loudspeaker. "... One."

Right on cue, Aunty Entity's voice blared out: "For God's sake, what now?"

Master turned toward Entity's lowered periscope and shouted, "Who run Bartertown?"

"Damn it!" Entity's voice shouted, raw with anger. "I told you—no more embargos."

Master sniggered again and spoke into Blaster's ear horn. "More."

Blaster gave the wheel another turn. Now the lights in Underworld began to dim. Even the pigs fell silent.

Master looked back at the periscope. "Who run Bartertown?" he cried.

Silence.

"Who run Bartertown?" Master repeated.

Standing in her bright, airy penthouse high above Bartertown, high above the Underworld, her fists clenched until her nails dug into her palms, Entity forced the words out of her throat. "You know who. . . ."

"Say," Master insisted with vindictive satisfaction.

"MasterBlaster," Entity whispered.

Max watched, unable to do anything else, as Master's beak-nosed face split in a vicious grin. "Say loud," he ordered. He threw another switch on the instrument panel.

Up above, Entity took a deep breath. Master was going to pay for this. Goddamn him, he was going to pay in blood. . . . "MasterBlaster," she grated. She jerked around as her own voice, heavily amplified, boomed out across Bartertown. All over town the waiting traders and merchants looked up, their faces mirrors of incredulity.

Now Master's voice echoed out through the loudspeakers. "MasterBlaster what?"

Entity stood for a long moment before the periscope, forcing herself to control the helpless rage that turned her voice to rags. "MasterBlaster runs Bartertown." Her voice echoed and reechoed from the hovels and the high rock walls.

The crowds stood still a moment longer, all those who had any understanding of what was occurring gaping with disbelief at MasterBlaster's audacity.

Master was cackling now, shaking with delighted laughter. "Lift embargo!" he ordered. Slowly Blaster began to turn the wheel back. Underworld, and then Bartertown, rose from the dead; filled again with the throb of machinery coming to life, the hum and pulse of energy returning to light the caverns and tunnels . . . the buzz of gossip and speculation.

The Collector looked up as the tunnel lights flickered on, his pink face livid with outrage, furious tears trickling down his quivering cheeks. Entity *was* Bartertown, Entity was everything: the heart, the life of his world; he worshiped her, and he felt her humiliation as his own. MasterBlaster had to be stopped before his insane ego destroyed all that they had built here. He remembered the stranger; wondered fleetingly whether Max had somehow been the cause of this . . . whether he was really the solution to their problem or simply already another corpse.

Back in the Underworld, Max was on his way back to the workshop and his waiting vehicle—propelled along by Blaster's irresistible mass. They stopped again beside his dune buggy, and Blaster hauled him off his feet once more, to face Master's arrogant stare.

"You right," Master hissed, "you fairy, me strong. You want foot in face?"

Max shook his head, wincing.

"Disarm!" Master ordered. Max nodded in surrender, not having to fake his willingness. Blaster twisted him around to face his vehicle, lowering him to the ground again. Blackfinger and a knot of other technicians had already gathered, watching and waiting with bald curiosity as Max climbed into the buggy. Settling in behind its steering wheel—which felt strangely unfamiliar after months of straddling its engine—he put his hands on the wheel. His head came up as he heard his monkey screech somewhere across the room. Held in the arms of a technician, it struggled wildly as it saw him climb into the car. It thought he was leaving—leaving it behind. Searching the shadowed cavern, Max spotted the monkey, gave it the signal to stay. Neither one of them was leaving Bartertown . . . yet.

The technicians crowded around like nervous brides, watching with mixed fear and fascination as Max pried up the hub in the center of the steering wheel. As he flipped the hub open the sudden shriek of an alarm sent them all diving away again, ducking for whatever cover they could find. Everyone within hearing . . . except

Blaster. Max watched the faceless monster stagger around the shop in obvious agony, trying to block the end of his ear horn while Master clung desperately to his saddle.

Max flicked a switch next to a flashing red light on the panel, deactivating the self-destruct. The light winked out, the alarm stopped. Max watched as Blaster slumped to the floor, Master whispering frantically, inaudibly into his ear, as if he were soothing him.

Intrigued, Max reached out to reactivate the alarm . . . hesitated, pulling his hand back. He reached up to his throat instead, feeling for the leather thong he wore around his neck. He pulled the death's-head whistle that was one of the few possessions he had left out from inside his T-shirt. Turning slightly away from Master's view, he put it to his lips and blew as Blaster began to pick himself up from the floor.

An earsplitting squeal filled the room; Blaster reeled in pain, collapsing again, clawing at his ear horn. Max stuffed the whistle away inside his shirt.

In the moment of silence that followed Blaster climbed inexorably to his feet and started back toward the dune buggy. But the car was empty. Max had disappeared.

Master looked sharply from side to side, his face pinched and frowning. "Him lucky him not stay," he muttered, burying his chagrin at Max's escape, his concern over Blaster's vulnerability, in a deadly promise.

Suddenly Blackfinger reappeared from under the far side of the car, triumphantly brandishing several sticks of gelignite.

Master whooped with delight, forgetting Max and his own anger as he realized that he had gotten what he had wanted, after all. The car was his, completely his; and he had plans for it. "Want air horns," he ordered eagerly, "mag wheels; foxtail..." A boyhood dream.

The technicians hesitated, exchanging dubious glances.

"No argue!" Master snarled, seeing their hesitation. "Go-fast stripes..."

Max stood well back in the shadows of the tunnel entrance and wiped his hand across his face; watching and listening as the technicians swarmed over his car, his own anger and relief tinged with a fleeting curiosity. But he had seen enough... He knew Blaster's weakness. He was through shoveling shit. He turned away.

And walked straight into Pig Killer.

Pig Killer gazed at him with open amazement. "Mister," he said, "what are you laying for?"

Max frowned, irritated at his own carelessness. "Nothing." He tried to push past the other man.

But Pig Killer stood his ground. "Who are you?" he asked, insistent.

'I ain't nobody," Max said wearily.

"No." Pig Killer shook his head, refusing to give in, his eyes bright with excitement. "I can feel it," he murmured. "The dice are rolling..." He spat into his hand and clenched it in a fist.

Max pushed past him wordlessly and strode away.

Pig Killer stood gazing at Max's retreating figure until the nearest Guard came up behind him and shoved him roughly back toward the pigs. "Back to work."

Pig Killer frowned. Glaring over his shoulder, he lifted his shovel and waded back into the pens.

Max entered Aunty Entity's penthouse for the second time, accompanied by Ironbar Bassey and two Guards. They had let him shower first—a luxury almost as rare as a piece of fresh fruit—and even supplied him with clean clothes before he paid her a second visit. He wore black leather pants and heavy jacket, a homespun shirt the color of ashes. Colors for a mourner. Leather lasted forever, and reminded him of a time when he had worn a uniform and that uniform had symbolized the law . . . to him, to the world. He assumed that their generosity was motivated less by altruism than by the fact that Entity didn't want pigshit on her carpets. Ironbar Bassey had thrown away his own ruined headdress; now he wore a Kabuki mask jammed on top of a stick, protruding from the back of his belt and rising over his shaven head like an ancestral totem.

Entity stood at the window as he entered, gazing out over her domain, lost in thought. There was no sign now that her living quarters had been a battleground earlier today. The Collector, sitting at her side and watching the doorway, reached up to touch her shoulder gently. Entity turned toward Max, asking the Question with her eyes.

"Okay," Max said, his own eyes like blue ice. He strode across the carpet to stand beside her. "I want my camel team, my monkey, and my vehicle."

Entity smiled. She spat in her hand, held it out to him. Max did the same. Their hands clenched together, sealing the deal and Blaster's death.

"You said a fair fight," Max murmured, thinking of what he had seen in the Underworld. There was no way it could happen there. "How?"

"As provided by the law." The Collector rose to his feet, gesturing toward the window.

Entity led Max to the far side of the penthouse where they could look down on a large open dome built of heavy metal scaffolding. "Thunderdome," she said. Max stared at the dark, silent cage. "Where men fight hand-to-hand,

cheek-to-jowl . . ." The words had the ring of steel and
the feel of a ritual about them. "There's no jury, no
appeal, and no parole." She looked up at him. "Two men
enter. One man leaves."

Behind her Ironbar and the Collector echoed the
words: "Two men enter. One man leaves."

Max glanced away at them, back at Entity. "Weapons?" he asked.

"Anything's   possible."   She   shrugged.   "Chance
decides."

Max noded, looking down at the arena again. "This
Thunderdome—how do I get in?"

She smiled. "That's easy. Pick a fight. Challenge him."
Her cool gaze searched his face, suddenly both penetrat-
ing and eager, as if she were trying to see what secret lay
behind his eyes; see what he saw; see into the future . . . .

Max turned away from the piercing scrutiny of her
stare. He headed for the elevator, and the Guards
followed.

CHAPTER 5

SATURDAY NIGHT

The welcome coolness of another night settled over Bartertown with the setting of the sun. The streets and stalls still bustled with trading activity as they did twenty-four hours a day under the day-bright glow of electric lights, but the dealing, like the air, was less feverish now. Two Imperial Guards stood at their post on top of the bell tower, their eyes roving the maze below calmly but ceaselessly.

Their heads jerked up in unison as the tower's loud-speakers, which had humiliated their leader earlier today, suddenly began to blast out loud and crazy music. Across the street a neon sign framed by strobe lights came to life with blinding brilliance. MasterBlaster had proclaimed

SATURDAY NIGHT.

Beneath it, more words flashed on and off:

LIVE! . . . LIVE! . . .

Down below, a gap-toothed codger in an eye patch looked up and whooped with excitement, ran off down the street like a lunatic, screeching, "Saturday Night!"

The Guards looked at each other, grinning, as down below more and more traders and locals turned and looked up, peered out through shutters and curtained doorways and down from roofs as the excitement spread like a fever. All over town, as the cry rang out and the music blared, the normally placid citizens of Bartertown dropped what they were doing—literally—and went on holiday.

In the Atomic Café the head cook/waiter dumped a steaming platter of stew onto the long trestle table and into the laps of the hungry traders and travelers as he bolted toward the ruined bus's doorway and out. Down the street the dentist/blacksmith, hovering over his latest patient/victim and drilling for oil, flung his drill away and ran off, leaving his howling patient thrashing helplessly, still strapped in the chair. Everywhere locals poured out of doorways and stalls, slid down pipes or scrambled up ladders, abandoning their work for a night where anything short of murder was not only permitted but encouraged. Dr. Dealgood stood on his balcony, flanked by Tweedledum and Tweedledummer, and raised a glass of wine in a toast to the good news: a night of pleasure and entertainment . . . and, perhaps later, some interesting repercussions.

And high above, Entity stood at her penthouse window, staring out at the spreading pandemonium, her face set and grim, her fist clenched over the gauze of the drawn-back curtain. "That's the fourth Saturday Night this week...." The words dripped acid. The Saturday Nights were Master's whim, turning Bartertown's world upside down, turning her disciplined and orderly city into an orgy of sex, drugs, and petty violence. Entity had tolerated it because she knew that Bartertown would never last unless its volatile population was allowed to blow off steam in some reasonably controlled way. But MasterBlaster was out of control....

It was hard to remember now that there had been a time when they had worked together as comrades, even friends—forging this town out of chaos, creating something of value, forcing civilization to live again in the middle of this wasteland. She had needed his technical expertise, and he had needed her vision to direct it; they had been the perfect team. But once the dream had been accomplished, once their power was secure, the balance hadn't been enough. He had wanted more, but it was *her* dream, her vision, her Law ... her town. She still needed his brain, but she would *not* let his raging egomania destroy all she had created here. Tonight would be the last time he mocked her rule....

Master would be none the wiser. He would never know that he'd been set up. And with Blaster gone, he would have to turn to her for help. She would be magnanimous, let him think she shared his grief....

She had done the right thing, hiring the stranger to challenge him. If anyone could defeat Blaster, he was the one. Her mouth twisted with a bitter smile. He was the one she had been waiting for. On the surface he was nothing, just one more wretched survivor, ragged, half crippled, burned out, but still he had beaten her best warriors. He hadn't done it on strength alone.

She had not gotten to the place where she stood now

without being a shrewd judge of character. She knew
how to pick a man she could rely on . . . and there was
something at the core of the stranger that was rarer than
diamonds—and as hard, as clear, as perfect. He would do
what had to be done, not simply because he was a man
who had no choice but because, strangely, he was a man
of honor. And then he would go on his way, because
somehow she knew there was nothing here that he
wanted. . . .

After tomorrow Bartertown would be secure again;
and hers alone again. She would never even know who
the stranger was, and she wanted to keep it that way. It
was better if she didn't know too much . . . better for both
of them. Because he aroused her curiosity; he aroused
her. . . .

She turned away from the spectacle below, back into
the inviolate space of her penthouse. The Collector stood
waiting patiently, his face filled with helpless frustration
as he listened to the shouts and screams echoing up from
the streets below. He was a good man, unlikely as he was:
completely devoted, one of her best. She shook her head
sadly and smiled; touched his arm with a reassuring hand
as she walked away.

Down in the marketplace Ironbar Bassey sat in a bar
with half a dozen of the Imperial Guards, casually
watching the crowd of revelers drinking, whooping, and
committing obscene acts right in front of his eyes. He
downed another drink of his own, tugging absently at his
feather earring. This was the perfect setup; it was only a
matter of time. Ironbar frowned, glancing back over his
shoulder as he heard a commotion louder than all the rest
coming fast in his direction. He slid down from his stool,
nodding to his men to follow.

Between the ramshackle buildings of a side alley came

Max's revamped dune buggy, careening wildly, its air horn blasting. At Master's order it had been fitted with a huge methane cylinder and totally souped up: mag wheels, flashing lights, foxtail streamers. Blaster sat in the driver's seat, operating the pedals. Master perched in his lap, swigging at a bottle of booze, wielding the steering wheel with wild and hopeless incompetence; spreading terror through the population of Bartertown as he roared down its streets. "Foot down!" he shouted into the ear horn, and Blaster stomped harder on the accelerator. Master laughed like a teenage maniac, loving every minute of it as the buggy veered and slewed, sending revelers diving for cover in all directions. The wild-haired blonde sitting on the seat beside him shrieked and giggled.

In the back of the vehicle Blackfinger the mechanic and a couple of hysterically laughing girls gyrated and staggered, hanging on for their lives as they swilled pure alcohol from a large, full drum. MasterBlaster circled Thunderdome, tires screeching, nearly running over two Imperial Guards crazy enough to try to slow him down. He smashed into their parked vehicle, caromed on across the street and into the eatery near Entity's tower. The car tore though the canvas wall, scattering food and people indiscriminately; crashed rear end first into a wagonload of barrels on the far side of the tent.

The car sat motionless, shrouded in the ruins of the cook tent. A crowd began to gather as their curiosity overcame their fright.

Abruptly the flame of a blow torch ate its way through the heavy canvas, charring a wider and wider hole, until the tent fell away, revealing the wildly laughing people inside.

"Happy Hour!" Blackfinger shouted. "Free booze!"

He began to ladle it out to the crowd, the two women helping him with giggling gusto.

Max stepped forward, pushing his way to the front of the crowd, holding out a jar. As Blackfinger filled the jar with alcohol Max's monkey leapt out of Blaster's arms and up onto the headrest, skittering toward its owner. Startled, Blaster jerked on the monkey's leash, dragged it screeching back again.

Max stepped forward and pitched the full jar of alcohol straight at Blaster's helmet. It struck with a splash, spraying liquor over both Blaster and Master. Blaster dropped the leash in surprise.

Max caught up his pet, holding it against his chest, soothing it. Master turned, his eyes blazing, to see the man who had mocked him and gotten away with it only this afternoon.

"Tell your ape to leave my monkey alone," Max said with deadly calculation.

Around him the laughing crowd abruptly fell silent as the revelers stared at him with sudden astonishment and fear.

Master slapped the side of his head in mock disbelief. "Hearing wonky," he said. "Sound like 'ape.'"

Max nodded, unflinching. "That's right. Ape."

The crowd began to back away from him as fear began to dominate. Anybody who talked to MasterBlaster like that must be crazy . . . worse than crazy, suicidal.

MasterBlaster moved across the seat, drawing closer to Max and to the uncertain crowd.

"Jumpin' Jesus," Master cried, looking out at the crowd, playing to the watchers now, "him sad." He pointed at Max. "Brain broken. Me explain." Looking back at Max, he said, "This Blaster." He patted the giant's shoulder. "He back snapper. Ball cracker. Death on foot. Savvy?"

"Yeah," Max said sourly. "Sounds just like an ape." He turned his back on them and began to walk away though the gaping onlookers.

"*Banzai*!" Master shouted into Blaster's ear horn, scrambling onto his back.

Blaster lunged forward, his hand shooting out to grab Max around the neck, dragging him back to the vehicle. With his free hand Blaster began to pry the monkey loose from Max's stubborn grasp. Max let go as the monkey screamed in pain; found himself helpless in Blaster's monstrous grip for the second time in one day. Blaster's hands began to tighten around his throat, forcing his head back. He glanced left and right, beginning to sweat, searching the crowd. *Where the hell was Bassey*?

"Three seconds," Master hissed fiercely, leaning close to Max's face. "Break neck. One . . . two . . ."

Abruptly a bristling armory of crossbows, clubs, harpoons, and spears surrounded them. The Collector and Ironbar Bassey stepped forward, flanked by half a dozen of the Imperial Guards, all with weapons ready. Slowly Blaster's grip loosened around Max's neck.

"MasterBlaster!" Ironbar rasped, in a voice ruined that morning by a flying platter. "Listen to the law!" The Collector pointed up at Entity's penthouse. Entity stood on the platform high above, its curtain wall drawn back as she looked down impassively on all that happened below.

"Aunty," Ironbar yelled up to her. "Two men in dispute."

"These our witness, Aunty," Master shouted, waving a hand at the crowd. "Us suffer bad. Want justice. Want Thunderdome."

Entity put her hands on her hips. "You know the law." She shouted the ritual warning. "Two men enter. One man leaves. . . ."

"Two men enter . . ." the crowd around Max murmured, like a sigh. "One man leaves."

"This *Blaster*!" Master yelled scornfully from the crook of the giant's arm. "Twenty men enter. Only him leave."

Entity shrugged. "Then it's your choice. Thunderdome." From somewhere beside her she raised a crossbow and fired a flaming arrow. The arrow arced high above the heads of the crowd, struck a lever on the roof of Thunderdome. The lever fell; a huge neon sign flickered to life above the crowd:

THUNDERDOME

The crowd looked up and burst into cheers. Max heard the cheer spread like a wave, rolling away through the streets of Bartertown. "Thunderdome! Thunderdome!" The crowds pressed around him, laughing and shouting, pummeling him in congratulation for having the complete insanity to provide them with the best entertainment a Saturday Night could provide—the opportunity to watch Blaster reduce a live human being to raw meat. The crowd swept on past him, breaking into a run as the townspeople and traders raced ahead for the choicest spots to view the coming massacre.

MasterBlaster roared off in the dune buggy, eager for the bloodletting, completely confident that the only blood anyone would see tonight was Max's.

Max stood where he was for a long moment, the only man in Bartertown without a smile on his face. Suddenly his head felt light, his throat tight; his heart was pounding. He looked down; in the palm of his hand lay the skull-faced whistle. He clenched his fist over it. Slowly he began to walk, following the crowd toward Thunderdome.

CHAPTER 6

THUNDERDOME

Under the lurid glare of flashing neon the citizens of
Bartertown swarmed to Thunderdome, swarmed up and
over it like ants, until the grid of steel pipes that caged
the arena was a seething mass of bodies. The space it
enclosed was more than large enough for two men to
engage in mortal combat while letting almost everyone in
town witness it. At Entity's order, even convicts and
slaves were given time off from their labors to watch
Bartertown's favorite spectacle, which was both instruc-
tional and highly entertaining.

Pig Killer, chained together in a line with the three
Hare Krishnas, peered through Thunderdome's metal
gridwork with mingled curiosity and foreboding as the
slaves took their reserved spot along the dome's south
side. Word had it that somebody had challenged Blaster,
which meant that somebody was as good as dead. But the

strange events he had witnessed this afternoon in the
Underworld were still fresh in his mind, and he couldn't
shake the premonition that he knew who the challenger
was going to be. There was something in the stranger's
face when he had watched MasterBlaster . . . Pig Killer
wasn't sure why the feeling was caught in his gut, any
more than he knew why he believed that something had
begun this afternoon that was not meant to end simply
with the stranger's corpse lying dead at Blaster's feet
tonight.

He looked up as a murmur spread through the crowd.
Aunty Entity appeared on the platform of her penthouse
high above the dome. Holding a flying fox between her
outstretched arms like a hang glider, she leaped from the
platform, soaring down toward Thunderdome in a flamboyant display of nerve and skill. She landed with precise
grace in the royal box on the far side of the area, the only
seating that actually opened directly onto the scene of
combat. Ironbar Bassey and the Collector were waiting
for her there, as usual; and tonight Master—without
Blaster—sat with them. The crowd looked toward her
expectantly.

"Welcome to another edition of Thunderdome," she
called out, her voice strong and resonant. Tonight her
presence seemed to crackle with an electric energy, as if
she focused the crowd's excitement like a lightning rod.

The crowd roared in answer, eager for the spectacle to
begin. Below, Dr. Dealgood bounded into the arena,
raising his top hat in salute and greeting. Tweedledum
and Tweedledummer sashayed into the ring behind him,
pulling a small cart that contained a full battery of
weapons for cutting, bashing, and spearing: knives, clubs,
a giant sledgehammer, even a chainsaw. As Dr. Dealgood
began to address the watchers his simpering assistants

passed the weapons up to members of the crowd, who
began to drop them onto platforms high up the walls of
the dome.

"Listen on . . . listen on! . . . " Dr. Dealgood shouted.
The crowd's racket began to fall away. "This is the truth
of it," he cried, repeating the words that he spoke before
every contest, fervent preacher and impassioned teacher
and cynical showman rolled into one. "Fighting leads to
killing, and killing gets to warring. And that was damn
near the death of us all. Look at us now, busted up and
everyone talkin' about hard rain. But we've learned. By
the dust of 'em all, Bartertown's learned." He paused for
breath, for effect, lowering his upraised arms. "Now
when men get to fighting, it happens here. And it finishes
here. Two men enter. One man leaves."

The crowd repeated his words like a credo: "Two men
enter. One man leaves."

Dr. Dealgood grinned, pure showman now, getting into
it, getting down to the part he really enjoyed. "And right
now I've got two men . . . two men with a gutful of fear.
Ladies and gentlemen, boys and girls—dying' time's
here." The crowd screamed its approval, louder than
before.

A gate at one end of the arena opened, and Dr.
Dealgood swung toward it with a flourish. "He's the back
snapper. The ball cracker. You know him. You love
him. . . ."

The crowd's cheers turned to boos and curses, already
anticipating the name he was about to speak.

"He's Blaster." Dr. Dealgood flung out his hand.
Blaster charged into the arena, still wearing his helmet
but with his body stripped down and oiled.

Dr. Dealgood turned back again, looking up at the
crowd. "The challenger—direct from out of the waste-

land. He's bad. He's beautiful. He's crazy." He shook his
head pityingly. "It's—" He broke off, his face suddenly
going slack as he realized that he had forgotten the
challenger's name. "It's . . . the man with no name . . . "
He waved vaguely at the opposite side of the arena.

Max entered the arena, still wearing the clothes he had
worn on the street. Leather held up better than skin in a
fight. He stopped just inside the arena, looking up at the
crowd. They stared down at him in utter silence. Then,
from somewhere across the arena, he heard one rousing
cheer. Pig Killer rattled his chains against the grid of
Thunderdome, cheering for the man in black; the Hare
Krishnas gazed at him uncomprehendingly. Max's
expression did not change.

Two Guards came forward, each carrying a harness.
The harnesses were suspended from bungeys—two coils
of   heavy,   elasticized   cable   suspended   from
Thunderdome's roof. Max let his eyes rove the arena, his
uncertainty growing as the Guard hitched him into the
harness. At last he located their weapons—on the platforms high up on the dome walls. He grimaced, beginning to understand. It didn't matter what you had
expected something to be, because it was never what you
expected. Usually it was worse. He wiped his hand across
his mouth.

As the Guards harnessed the two men to their bungeys,
more figures burst into the arena. Max stared as the
crowd came alive again. What he saw could only be
cheering squads. There were two sets of them, the first
made up of the most strikingly attractive employees of
the Palace of Dreams, wearing peekaboo costumes that
amply displayed their charms. Linking arms, they began
a clumsy and vaguely obscene tap-dance routine, singing
loudly, "Hustle, Blaster! Hustle, Blaster! Go! Go! Go!"

The second squad, led by an immensely fat balloon of a woman, seemed to have been chosen strictly for ugliness. They carried letter cards, intended to spell out the message, "GO MAX!" Having apparently been selected for brains as well as looks, they held up a message that read instead, "OG! MAX." It took them several tries to get it right.

Max stood impassively, ignoring the grotesque spectacle as he ignored the crowd's laughter. Let them have their joke; it was all meaningless, anyway. Humiliation was nothing compared to pain. . . . He glanced up at the weapon caches again, down at Blaster; forcing himself to breathe slowly and deeply, to stay calm. You did what you had to, endured what you had to. When had anybody ever had another choice?

He was jerked out of his thoughts as the bungey he was attached to suddenly pulled taut above him, yanking him off his feet. He hung suspended, his feet just off the ground, dangling like a side of beef. Looking up, he saw that the same thing had happened to Blaster.

Dr. Dealgood stepped forward between them, addressing them both. "Thunderdome's simple. Get to the weapons—use 'em any way you can." He smiled sardonically. "I know you won't break the rules. . . . there aren't any." He backed away again, hurrying toward the exit. The cheering squads had reached the gate before him and were already scuttling out. One of the waiting Guards caught Max's harness from behind, hauling him back toward one side of the dome. The other Guard was doing the same to Blaster.

Aunty Entity rose to her feet, and the crowd's restless murmur hushed once more. She turned to gaze down at the two combatants, her face serene, her voice shadowed. "Remember where you are," she murmured like a benediction. "This is Thunderdome, and death's listening. He'll take the first man who screams." She raised her hands.

At her signal the Guards let go of the two men, heaving them back toward the center of the arena with a rough shove.

Max sailed toward Blaster, his movements completely out of his control. Their bodies slammed together with a teeth-jarring thud, rebounded; Max spun helplessly on the end of his bungey. Blaster arced forward again, completely in control at the end of his own cable. His huge, open hand smacked into the side of Max's head, twirling him like a top. Blaster smacked Max again, set him spinning faster.

The arena flashed past in a nauseating blur. Giddy with vertigo, tasting blood, Max saw Blaster's helmet blink past in front of him again, heard the giant's inhuman, echoing laughter. It was a nightmare in zero gravity . . . there were no rules at all, just like Dr. Dealgood had promised—not even the rules of nature. Desperately Max thrust out his arms, holding them rigid. First one fist, and then the other, smashed into Blaster's side. Max swore; it was like hitting a stone wall. As the impact jarred his spinning body to a halt, Blaster lunged forward, utterly unaffected by the blows. His trunklike arms clamped around Max in a bear hug and began to tighten. Max squirmed and kicked, his arms pinned uselessly at his sides, his feet striking air; the crushing vise of Blaster's murderous embrace closed around him like the arms of Death. His head swam; he felt his eyes bulging out of their sockets . . . saw the throbbing veins bulge in Blaster's straining throat.

Twisting his head, Max sank his teeth into Blaster's neck. Blood spurted into his face, but still the bone-cracking pressure kept wringing the life out of him. He bit deeper, in a frenzy of desperation.

Blaster's grip spasmed and released him; the giant's clawing hands tore at him as Max pried and kicked his way free, pushing off from Blaster's chest, bouncing away . . . losing all control of his motion again.

Blaster lunged after him, grabbed him by the shoulders, and hurled him at the far wall. Max cried out as he smashed into the iron bars, hands flung up, eyes shut; the darkness behind his eyelids exploded into pain-stars as he crashed against the grille, caromed away.

Blaster caught him again as he sailed past and heaved him onward like a human football. Spectators scrambled this time as they saw him coming. He crashed into the opposite wall with a grunt of pain; tasted fresh blood as he bit his own tongue. But this time he was ready for the crash; he made a frantic grab for the bars, managed to wrap his fingers through the grille and jerk himself to a halt, stopping his spin-dizzy, headlong flight. Forcing air into his spasming lungs, he shook the blood and sweat from his eyes, looking back into the arena. "A fair fight," Entity had said. It had to be a fair fight in Thunderdome. Blaster knew the ropes here, literally, and he was as out of his depth as a cat that had fallen into a shark tank. He'd forgotten to ask Entity, "Fair to who?"

Blaster launched off from his place at the arena's center, lifting his legs as he headed toward Max like a cannonball.

Max held his place grimly, waiting . . . rolled aside on the grille at the last instant, dodging sideways.

Blaster crashed into the metal bars this time; they groaned and buckled under the impact. Max scrambled on up the dome, heading for the nearest weapons platform. Blaster was human, even if he didn't act like it. He

bled like any normal man . . . he could be killed like any
normal man. Max blocked out the pain of his screaming
body with fierce concentration, sharply aware of his every
move and Blaster's; knowing that if he gave in to pain or
panic now, he was the dead one, not Blaster.

The weapons cache was just above him. He was almost
there; he could see the blades of half a dozen different
weapons shining like stars. He reached up, straining
closer . . . closer . . . his hand closed over the haft of the
machete.

Blaster leaped; his own hand grabbed Max's ankle as
he let go of the bars, jerking Max down with all of his
freefalling weight. The blade spun out of Max's hand,
thudding into the dust halfway across the arena as the
two men fell together. They reached the limit of the
bungeys . . . rebounded like a yo yo, hitting the roof . . .
fell again . . . bounced up again.

As their momentum slowed Blaster let go of Max and
leaped, catching hold of a bar high up on the dome. He
swung himself toward another weapons platform as Max
continued to fall helplessly. Blaster grabbed the sledgehammer and a knife, launched off again from the platform, swinging the hammer like a battle-ax.

Max turned, spiraling in the air, and saw the hammer
coming. He twisted, swinging his feet; bounced aside as
the sledgehammer sailed past, missing him by bare
inches.

Max caught hold of the grid again, scrambled up it
after the remaining weapons. Blaster hurled the knife.
Looking back, Max lunged upward, trying to escape its
fatal trajectory . . . not high enough. The knife that had
been heading for his chest was aiming for his groin
instead. He kicked out wildly, lifting his legs.

The knife whistled between them, struck home in the

throat of a spectator clinging to the grid behind him. The man next to the sudden corpse laughed in hysterical surprise; a high, yodeling laugh that Max recognized instantly. There couldn't be two laughs like that in the middle of this desert . . . not two in the world. Max swung around, for the first time getting a clear look at the man who had robbed him, the man who was responsible for all of this. There was no recognition whatsoever in the other man's eyes. But he had no time to renew old acquaintances now. He jerked the bloody knife from the dead man's throat and spun back, readying himself for Blaster's new attack.

Blaster came flying at him, swinging the hammer. Max rolled across the bars again, out of his path.

Behind the grille, Jedediah recoiled in sudden horror. The hammer clanged against the bars, missing his fingers by inches. Max grinned mirthlessly, slashing at Blaster with the knife—missing him as Blaster let go of the grid, ducking expertly. But the knife grazed the top of Blaster's helmet as he sprang away, cutting the bungey almost through. It parted under Blaster's weight; Max watched him plummet to the ground.

Max leaped after him, more confident now, beginning to get the feel of this bizarre mode of battle. He swung down to the arena floor, slashing at Blaster again, hacking away half of his ear horn. Soaring up and away, Max turned back again, swooping recklessly down for another attack.

But this time Blaster was on his feet and ready. The giant swung the sledgehammer, let it go, sent it arcing through the air. . . .

Max twisted like an eel, but this time there was no escape. The hammer slammed into his stomach, cracking ribs, doubling him up with a cry of agony. The knife flew from his hand. Blaster hit him a moment later, hurtling against Max with all his weight, dragging him down. Max's bungey snapped; they crashed down on the hard-packed earth together.

Max lay sprawled on the ground, retching with pain, unable to move as Blaster picked himself up again and started slowly toward him, the hammer raised.

All at once Max remembered the thing his reeling brain had forgotton for far too long . . . almost forever. Pushing himself up, he dug frantically inside his torn shirt, pulling out his secret weapon. He pushed the skull-faced whistle between his bloody lips and blew.

An earsplitting screech echoed across the arena. Blaster clamped his hands to his ear horn, dropping the sledgehammer, swaying on his feet as the shrill tone reverberated inside his helmet.

Master, perched beside Entity in the royal box, scrambled up from his seat in sudden fear as Max lunged forward on hands and knees, catching up the hammer. Staggering to his feet, Max raised the hammer and lurched forward through a haze of pain. Swinging it down, he struck Blaster's helmet from behind with a resounding *bong*. The hammer glanced off the metal, barely denting it. Blaster spun around, as if he hadn't felt the blow at all, and wrenched the hammer from Max's shaking hands.

Holding the whistle between his clenched teeth, Max blew again.

Blaster recoiled, dropped the hammer. Max picked it up. He blew the whistle over and over, driving Blaster backward while he found the strength to make his brutalized body lift the hammer for another blow. Swinging the sledgehammer up, he smashed it down on Blaster's head again, driving him to his knees. Blaster stayed there this

time, stunned. Max swung once more, a sideways blow
that knocked the giant sprawling to the ground.

Max reeled forward, leaning on the sledgehammer like
a crutch, supporting his rubbery legs. His own broken,
bleeding body wanted nothing more than to fall on its
face beside the Blaster's. He held himself on his feet by
sheer willpower, knowing that Blaster wasn't finished yet,
even if he was; that he had to finish the giant now or he
never would . . .

Blaster rolled forward, already struggling up again. He
slumped into a sitting position, shaking his head. Dimly
Max could hear Master screaming from the stands, "Up,
Blaster! Up! Up!"

Max swung the hammer up and back with the last rags
of his strength, sweeping it around for a savage uppercut.
It crashed into Blaster's head, ripping the helmet from its
straps, sending it sailing up toward the roof as Blaster's
body was flung backward by the impact. The crowd
gasped, seeing the helmet flying skyward, a body lying
motionless below . . . with no visible head. The helmet
clanged off the roof of Thunderdome, fell to the ground
again, lay spinning like a top. Master covered his face
with his hands as beside him in the box the Collector
grimaced and Ironbar Bassey smiled. Entity looked on in
grim silence, her face revealing nothing.

In the arena Max stood motionless, dazed with shock,
as he watched the spinning helmet slow. It slithered to a
stop, lay still in the dirt; with mingled relief and dismay
he saw that it was empty. Clenching his teeth, he lurched
toward Blaster's inert body, his legs trembling, his hands
slippery with sweat and blood. Barely able to drag the
hammer with him this time, he wondered how in the
name of hell he would ever lift it off the ground again.
But this time the blow *would* be the last; the blow that

saved his own life and gave him back a future. He knew he would find the strength somewhere . . . . Around him now the crowd's voice was rising, chanting, "Two men enter, one man leaves!"

Step by step he closed with Blaster's body; the journey across ten feet of bloodstained ground seemed to take a hundred years. He reached Blaster's motionless feet, looked on along the inert body toward his head. Blaster's face was hidden beneath his upflung arm; Max still couldn't see what he looked like. Gritting his teeth, Max lifted the hammer with shaking arms. This time it wouldn't take much; this time . . .

Blaster stirred; his hand slid away from his face, rose in sudden protest as the giant's eyes flickered open and he saw the hammer in Max's grip.

Max froze, the hammer raised over his head, his own face filling with stunned disbelief. Before him now was not the face of a monster but only the innocent and incomprehending stare, the faintly distorted features of a severely retarded young man. Max stared a moment longer. Then, slowly, his rigid muscles let go, the hammer dropped onto his shoulder. He stood motionless where he was, without the strength to move, his own mind a blank as he tried desperately to force himself to start thinking again.

Master scrambled down out of the royal box, scurried across the arena and past Max to Blaster's side with all the speed his short legs could give him. The crowd had fallen silent again, curious, waiting. Still standing in the royal box, Entity broke the silence, calling out to Max, her words warning and goading: "Two men enter. One man leaves."

On the ground beside Blaster, Master turned to look up at Max, tearing off his helmet, pulling off his goggles.

"He don't know," Master said, his voice quavering, his eyes pleading. "Him just child. This my fault." He cradled Blaster's head in his arms, stroking the battered face tenderly. Blaster stared up at him with dazed incomprehension.

"You know the law." Entity's voice cut sharply across Master's pleading, addressing Max; urging, threatening.

"This is Thunderdome," the Collector shouted.

"Kill him!" Ironbar snarled.

Max stared at the two men before him, one lying helplessly on the ground, the other crouched beside him . . . one without a normal body, one without a normal mind. Neither one of them could have survived alone in this pitiless post-holocaust world where any weakness marked a man as a victim. Only together, in that incredible symbiosis, had they been able to survive and even triumph.

Max looked up at Entity again and shook his head. He lowered the hammer. "No," he said. "This wasn't part of the deal."

Master looked up sharply from Blaster's side. "Deal?" he snapped. "What mean, deal?" He scrambled to his feet, looking toward the royal box.

Entity rose from her seat, leaning forward over the edge of the box, ignoring Master as she stared at Max in incredulous disbelief. He couldn't. He *couldn't* be refusing her now! Not now, not when he had actually beaten Blaster; when, with one more blow, the one thing she had begun to believe she would never achieve would be accomplished. He couldn't be standing there refusing, revealing her treachery to the entire town. Not the man who could give her what she wanted, the man who *had* . . . She would have given him anything, anything he'd asked for! Her white-knuckled fingers clenched over the rail.

Max's pale eyes turned back her unspoken demand with the impassive coldness of a glacier. The same diamond-hard thing that lay at the core of his soul, the strength she had sensed that made her believe he would succeed, had turned against her when he realized the truth; and she was as certain as she had been then that he would never obey her command now. "You must have tasted it," she murmured. "It was in your hand—you had everything." By all the devils in hell, only a saint or a madman would look at her that way . . . and she was equally certain that the warrior was no saint.

Max threw down the hammer and turned his back on her. He stumbled wordlessly away toward the gate.

Master started after him, his small face pinched with fury. "Say!" he demanded, his fists clenching "What deal!" Max did not answer. Master spun back to face Entity, his eyes darkening as his own suspicion suddenly gave him the answer. "Me stupid," he said slowly, loudly enough for all the arena to hear. "Me see now. You got heart of darkness. This place finish." He waved his hand, trembling with fury, and Entity knew that he would keep his promise.

Beside her, Ironbar Bassey stepped forward and raised his crossbow; she made no move to stop him. "No," Ironbar rasped. "We've just started." Grinning, he fired twice; both bolts struck Blaster squarely in the chest. The crowd gasped with one voice as Entity's chief enforcer murdered her Law.

Almost to the gate, Max jerked around at Master's cry of horror. He watched the little man rush back to Blaster's side as Blaster crumpled in the dust.

"Who run Bartertown now?" Ironbar's voice shouted,

mocking them from the box. He turned back to Entity with a twisted grin of speculation on his face; his smile faded as it met her own face, a mask of bitterness and disgust.

Master crouched over Blaster's bloody corpse, his tiny hands clenched around a crossbow bolt, tugging futilely. But what had been done could not be undone: Blaster was dead. He buried his face against the dead boy's cheek, sobbing.

Max turned back again toward the exit gate, confronting the two armed Guards posted beyond it. "Open it."

The Guards stood with arms folded and did not move. Ironbar reloaded his crossbow, the smile back on his face, his eyes already on Max's back.

Max moved closer to the gate, caught hold of the bars, holding himself on his feet. "Open it!" he said again, his voice raw. The Guards stared at him, unmoving and unmoved.

On the far side of the dome Pig Killer shouted, "Two men entered. *One man leaves.*"

Standing on the ground now beside him, Jedediah picked up the chant. He had no idea whose life he was shouting for, any more than he cared what sort of dirty deal the man had made with Entity. He only knew that he had seen a damn good fight. Any man who could bring Blaster down deserved to come back and fight another time.

Others in the crowd began to pick up the cry; the chant began to echo around the arena: "Two men entered. *One man leaves. One man leaves!*" They banged and rattled the bars of Thunderdome until the whole arena was calling for the survivor's freedom. Max stood unmoving before the gate, the taste of blood still in his mouth, the crowd's demand echoing hollowly in his ears as he waited for the decision he knew would be made only in the royal box behind him ... waiting for the searing pain of a crossbow bolt in his back.

Ironbar moved forward, oblivious to the crowd's roar as he took aim at Max. The Collector's arm reached out suddenly, forcing his weapon down. Entity stood rigidly, frowning as her eyes roamed the howling crowd. She couldn't kill the stranger in cold blood now; another murder and the crowd would riot. But she was goddamned if she was going to let that son of a bitch bust their deal and go free!

All at once she moved, her decision made. She leaped down from the royal box to land in the arena. Turning on the crowd, fury blazing in her eyes, she prowled along the base of the dome, glaring out at the watchers like an angry lioness; commanding their attention, their silence. The stranger had betrayed her trust, broken his word; revealed her plan to everyone in Bartertown and, worst of all, made her directly responsible for causing Blaster's death. Ironbar Bassey was the one who had pulled the trigger; but he was her right hand ... it might as well have been her own hand. The stranger was *not* getting away without paying for that.

"You think I don't know the Law?" she shouted. She raised her arms, on fire now with messianic fervor. "Wasn't it me who wrote it? And I say now"—she flung out her hand, sent an accusing finger at Max like an arrow—"this man has broken the law. Right or wrong, we had a deal. And the law says: Bust a deal, face the wheel."

The crowd was hushed now, turning away from Max, all eyes fixed on her. At last even Max turned back to face her, his own face resigned, no resistance left in his body as he felt the tide of the crowd's support ebbing away from him, flowing back to Entity. As her words rang out the watchers began to pick up the refrain, chanting the new ritual response: "Bust a deal, face the wheel."

The two Guards came through the gate and caught Max from behind. Max did not struggle, too beaten and too exhausted to resist, even if he had been stupid enough to try. They held him where he was at the side of the arena, waiting; he watched mutely, almost past caring, while new preparations were made.

Dr. Dealgood bounced back into the arena, supervising the change of attractions. This night was turning out even better than he'd anticipated. More Guards led his milk-white stallion, his trademark, into the arena and harnessed it to the dead body of Blaster. Straining with effort, the stallion began to haul Blaster's corpse feet-first out of Thunderdome. Master followed silently at Blaster's side, his face striken and streaked with tears, Blaster's one mourner in their bizarre funeral procession.

As Master trailed the body toward the gate two large, heavily muscled legs stepped in front of him, blocking his way. He looked up, his face filling with fear. Ironbar Bassey stood before him; his samurai helmet was already jammed onto the Guard's bald head. Ironbar grinned as he leaned down, plucking the small man off his feet. Holding Master in his arms like a helpless child, Ironbar stroked his cheek with gentle menace, crooning him a soft lullably filled with ugly threat as he carried him off across the arena.

Dr. Dealgood, trailed by Tweedledum and Tweedledummer, strode back into the center of Thunderdome, signaling for silence. Entity, back in the royal box again, looked on in silence as the hatchet-faced ringmaster began his new gig.

"Listen on . . . listen on!" Dr. Dealgood shouted. "Nothing's surer: All our lives hang by a thread." On cue the two Guards hustled Max forward into the center of the arena. "Now we got a man waiting for sentence." Dr. Dealgood said as Tweedledum waved her hand with a flourish, introducing Max as if he were a contestant in a game show.

"But ain't it the truth," Dr. Dealgood cried, "you take your chances with the law. Justice is only a roll of the dice, a flip of the coin, a turn of the wheel."

Tweedledummer pointed eloquently toward the roof of Thunderdome. An enormous wheel of fortune hung suspended there, a nearly perfect imitation of the kind once used on television game shows. Civilization might be dead on earth, but its memory lingered on. The wheel began to drop slowly into the arena. Below it hung a sign: WHEEL OF JUSTICE.

The wheel settled at last, waist-high between Max and Dr. Dealgood. The Guards shoved Max forward, Dr. Dealgood and the girls watching him expectantly.

Max stood woodenly, staring down at the wheel with dull eyes. A Guard grabbed his wrist, slapping his hand against the edge of the wheel to set it spinning. His choice of fates clattered past him in an unreadable blur; the wheel began to slow again as the rubber flipper at its edge batted against one raised spoke after another.

The words in their pie-slice sections grew readable again, passing more and more slowly, as the Wheel settled toward its judgment: LIFE IMPRISONMENT, SPIN AGAIN, FORFEIT GOODS, AUNTY'S CHOICE, UNDERWORLD. The crowd held its breath, unable to see what fate the flipper was clacking toward but knowing they would know it soon enough.

Entity stood frozen at the rail of her royal box, her face set, her eyes opaque, as if by the sheer force of her will she could cause it to choose the fate she would have chosen for the man waiting numbly below.

Max and the Guards, Dr. Dealgood, Tweedledum and Tweedledummer all stood side by side, barely breathing, as Justice clattered toward its final decision. Barely moving now, the Wheel quivered as the flipper toyed with ACQUITTAL. The flipper trembled against the final peg ... clicked once more into the next section: GULAG.

The vacuous smiles disappeared from the faces of Tweedledum and Tweedledummer, driven out by a look of utter horror.

"Gulag!" Dr. Dealgood shouted, his cadaverous face split in a grin as he stepped back to face the crowd.

All around the arena the watchers recoiled, whispering the word. Max turned to look at them as the flicker of hope inside him guttered out, as the whisper became a wailing chant that echoed around him like a banshee calling away souls, "Gulag ... gu-gu-lag ...."

What the hell was Gulag? He tried to force his dazed brain to remember, searching for a memory decades old: Something about banishment, exile ... disappearance.

Clinging to the bars of Thunderdome, Pig Killer shook his head, looking down in silent sorrow. Beside him Jedediah made the sign of the cross clumsily in the air.

And Ironbar Bassey smiled. Starting across the arena toward the gate, he jerked on the length of chain that trailed from his fist. At its other end, wearing a slave's metal collar and chained like a dog, Master huddled in grief and fear, his face buried in his hands. Ironbar dragged him from the arena, flaunting Master's helplessness and his own new power to the crowd; proving to Max the stupidity of his defiance, the pointless masochism of his punishment.

Max looked up at the royal box, saw the smile of pitiless satisfaction that pulled at Entity's lips, her lust for vengeance fed by the bitterness of her disappointment.

Around him the crowd's hungry voice swelled even louder: "Gulag! Gulag! Gulag!"

CHAPTER 7

GULAG

A new dawn broke over the Devil's Anvil; the sun climbed into the perpetually cloudless sky as it had done for eons, and would do for eons more, pouring its light down on the glittering bed of the dry lake. Reflected heat rose from the lifeless salt pan in shimmering waves.

The citizens and traders of Bartertown stood in straggling ranks along the precipice above, or scattered down the slope to the lakeshore, squinting and shielding their eyes as they looked out at the white wilderness of salt, at the scene unfolding below them. Jedediah stood on the hillside with the others, burdened down with the new propeller and the heavy load of trade goods he had bartered Max's belongings for—waiting with naked curiousity for a glimpse of one last Bartertown spectacle before he started on his solitary homeward journey. Below him, marking the beginning or the end of the

Devil's Anvil, thirty-two tall poles capped with skulls pointed skyward, like stark, bony fingers reaching toward heaven. A group of Guards stood silently on the lake bed, surrounding the spot where Entity waited beyond the poles, with Ironbar Bassey and Dr. Dealgood at her side.

Another Guard led an ancient, skeletal horse slowly down the embankment and between the poles. Max was tied to its saddle, his hands bound behind him—riding backward, forced to look back at everything he was losing as he was led away from Bartertown and all possibility of rescue. The Guard stopped the horse as he reached the place where Entity and the others stood. Max tore his gaze away from the watchers on the hill—from Jedediah standing there, free and loaded down with the goods bought with his sweat . . . with his life. Twisting his aching, battered body, he turned in the saddle to look over his shoulder and winced as the blinding furnace of the Devil's Anvil drove fingers of light into his eyes.

So this was Gulag, the fate that the Wheel and his own stubborn refusal had chosen for him. He looked down, blinking his dazzled vision clear, in time to see Entity step forward and pour a beaker of water into a glass flask hanging just in front of his horse's nose, suspended from what looked like a fishing pole lashed to his saddle.

Entity glanced up at him, feeling his gaze on her; her dark stare met his, as hard and impenetrable as obsidian. "One day's life," she said softly, "to remind you of what you've lost."

Dr. Dealgood pulled Max halfway out of the saddle, face-to-face with his own iron smile. "Death's found you, soldier." His grin widened in promise as he squinted into the light. "But he's gonna take you like a lover—hot and slow and full of pain."

Ironbar Bassey stepped forward, carrying a mask—a

hollow papier-mâché head painted with a leering clown face, the face of the twisted, mocking fate that ruled their lives . . . the face of a fool who had thrown his life away for nothing. He dropped the mask over Max's head, cutting off his vision, muffling sound. Max flinched and pulled back, sudden panic seizing him by the throat as the stifling darkness choked off his senses. He was jerked down again as hands bound the mask in place; the stabbing pain of his cracked ribs made him gasp.

Entity looked away from Max as Ironbar finished tying the mask on. Raising her voice again, she called out to the crowd, "Thirty-two poles to mark the passage of thirty-two men, all of them sentenced to the void . . . swallowed by the sand." She looked back at Max. "On this day it makes thirty-three."

She turned, glancing away as Ironbar unexpectedly pulled a branding iron from a brazier carried by one of his men. He stepped up to Max, grabbing him by the front of his jacket again. He pressed the branding iron into one of the mask's staring eyes, grinning as he watched it burn through toward the living eye beneath it. Max began to struggle uselessly.

Entity stepped forward, grasping Ironbar's wrist, forcing him to drop the iron.

Ironbar turned, glaring, his jaw twitching as he let go of Max. "Fair trade, Aunty," he rasped. "My voice, his eyes."

Entity stared at him without answering. Stepping back suddenly, she brought her hand around in a stinging whack on the horse's rump.

The horse bolted away, charging out onto the lake bed, the flask of water lapping tantalizingly in front of its nose. Entity, Ironbar, and Dr. Dealgood stood together in silence, watching it go. A funereal silence hung over the hillside as well, as the fleeing horse thundered away into the shining, lifeless wastes. The silence stretched until the horse and its helpless burden were nothing more than a speck in the vast, snowblind wilderness, until they disappeared like a mirage into the shimmering wall of heat. One by one the watchers began to turn away at last, muttering among themselves as they headed back for town.

The horse ran on for what seemed to Max's agonized body like years, every jarring thud of its hooves against the ground driving up through his bones like the blow of a sledgehammer, racking him with fresh pain. But at last the horse's mindless fright subsided, and its mindless flight slowed, dropping from a panic-stricken gallop to a canter, to a trot. Blowing hard, its flanks lathered white with sweat, it broke at last into a shambling walk. There was nothing now in any direction but the glittering sand, the sunlight glancing up from its mirror surface, doubling and redoubling its heat. . . . Nothing for the befuddled animal to do but keep on, hour after hour, aimlessly pursuing the promise of water that it scented always just ahead, never able to comprehend why the water remained forever out of reach.

On its back Max reeled in the saddle, his breath coming in shallow, suffocated gasps, his face drowning in sweat inside the oven that his mask had become. His own brain was barely more functional than the horse's as he sank into a stupor of sweltering misery. He twisted mechanically at the thongs that bound his wrists behind him, the only movement he was capable of, obsessed with freeing his hands the way the horse was obsessed by water. His wrists bled, already rubbed raw; the thongs had been knotted by an expert.

The sun reached its zenith and rolled on through its

endless dance. It sank below the horizon at last, bringing the night and a brief reprieve for the tortured creatures below. They struggled on through the darkness toward a new dawn while the ageless stars gazed down on the eternal land.

In Bartertown, miles behind them now, the blazing artificial stars of another night's day shone steadily, driving back the darkness, seeming as permanent and unfailing as the stars in the sky above. And then, abruptly, the lights flickered and dimmed, as somewhere in the Underworld a pipe broke apart at a critical seam, and critical pressure began to drop.

Ironbar Bassey, Underworld's new overlord, stood with two of his Guards, watching the pipe leak steam with snarling frustration. Ironbar turned back again to the heavy winch behind him. Master dangled from a harness at the end of its cable, above an enclosure full of pigs.

Ironbar pointed at the hissing pipe. "Fix it."

Master glared at him with all the defiance he could muster. "You run Bartertown," he said. "You fix."

Ironbar took hold of the winch. Slowly he began to lower Master into the pigs.

Unnoticed behind him, the periscope dropped from the ceiling, turning, searching. And farther in the shadows, Pig Killer stood silently, watching all that happened; he carried Max's monkey cradled in one arm and a full water bottle in his other hand.

Master's legs dropped until they dangled among the pigs. The grunting and snuffling below him increased in pitch as the pigs closed in, scenting fresh meat. Pigs would eat anything, as Master knew with terrifying certainty, even human flesh. And they weren't always particular about whether it was still moving. He shrieked in terror as their sharp tusks began to nip and pull at his unprotected legs. Grinning, ˉronbar lowered him farther.

"Me do! Me do!" Masteˇ screamed, wild with fear. He was touching ground now, facing a ring of pigs, each one of them outweighing him by hundreds of pounds. "No!" he cried hysterically, "Pull up! Please—pull up!"

"That's enough." Entity's voice rang out from the shadows, sharp with disapproval.

Ironbar turned, startled, as Entity herself emerged from the gloom. His mouth twisted. "I'll decide what's enough." His eyes burned, challenging her interference in his domain.

Entity stopped, her own eyes narrowing, her own mouth thinning at his arrogance. She had sensed this coming: He had wanted MasterBlaster's position; the corruption that went with the power was already infecting him. She would have to watch him more carefully, be ready to squash him if he got too dangerous. Men like Ironbar had their uses but they were a dime a dozen. He had none of Master's dedication to what had been created in Underworld or Bartertown. He wanted power for its own sake, because it let him do what he pleased. And seeing what pleased Ironbar Bassey did not please Entity. She curbed her anger and said only, "You want to use him or kill him? Get him up."

Ironbar turned back to the winch obediently; logic still had some hold over his instincts. He began to haul Master up.

Entity waited until Master was out of the pen, dangling at her eye level. "Do what Ironbar says, okay?" she asked him almost apologetically, almost ashamed. Her dark eyes did not stay long on his face.

Master nodded, his chest heaving, still speechless with fright. Entity turned away from the sight of him and strode back into the darkness. The Underworld was as much a part of her domain as Bartertown, as much hers as her own penthouse, but there was small satisfaction in being the queen of hell.

Pig Killer slipped deeper into the shadows as Entity and her bodyguards stalked past. Slipping away down a side tunnel, he found what he was really searching for. He climbed up a ladder and wormed his way into one of the ancient drainage tunnels that spewed seepage or sewage out onto the waiting desert; fumbled his way along its dark, dank length until he reached its end. A line of heavy iron bars stood across it like clenched teeth, too close together to let a man escape but wide enough for a monkey to slip through. Pig Killer pushed the monkey carefully between the bars. On its back it wore the tiny harness he had knotted together out of thongs. Quickly he fastened the water bottle to the harness.

He pointed out of the pipe's mouth and through the standing ranks of the funeral poles, toward the lake bed beyond; sent the monkey skittering off after Max's fading trail, running away into the night to find its master.

Pig Killer started back through the tunnel alone, knowing that if he was discovered wandering here he would catch bloody hell for it; worse, if Ironbar found out what he'd been up to. But he couldn't believe, after all he'd seen, that he'd really seen the last of Max . . . not if he could do anything to change it. Somehow, in spite of all he'd been through in his life, he couldn't shake the feeling that some men could make a difference in their own lives, or in the future. He hoped he was one of them; he knew the stranger was.

He slipped past the still-hissing pipe, taking advantage of the darkness. Master stood beside it again, cooperating now with pathetic willingness. Pig Killer hesitated,

watching as Master marked a cross on the broken pipe
with a piece of chalk. "Kick," he said, pointing at the
cross.

One of the Guards stepped forward and kicked the
pipe. Nothing happened; steam still hissed out in a white
cloud like before. Ironbar turned on Master with deadly
eyes, grabbing his chain and yanking him back toward
the pigs.

"Kick hard," Master insisted desperately. "Like
Blaster."

Ironbar pushed the Guard out of the way and smashed
his boot against the pipe. The steam diminished and
stopped as the loose pieces jumped back into place in
their coupling. One by one the lights of Bartertown and
Underworld began to flicker on again.

Ironbar released his grip on Master's chain, nodding in
satisfaction. He turned away, leaving Master lying
slumped next to the winch, unguarded. In Underworld
where was there to run to? Master knew better than
anyone that the answer was Nowhere. He lay where he
was, tears filling his eyes as he thought of what he had
done to himself, and worse, to Blaster, by his own arrogance and ruinous pride.

A hand reached out of the shadows, touching Master's
shoulder gently. Master started in terror, jerking away
from the touch. Looking up, he saw that the hand held
only a cup of water. A convict he didn't know and
wouldn't have remembered, anyway, leaned down beside
him with no malice on his face, only an inexplicably
respectful smile. "Drink. C'mon, Master," he urged
softly.

Master shook his head. "I'm not Master," he muttered. "My name is Elvis Ford. I'm thirty-five inches tall.
Sixty-six years old. And my life is over. . . ." For the first

time in longer than he could remember, he spoke like a normal human being and not in the pidgin English he had always used for Blaster's sake.

Pig Killer bent down and picked the small man up in his arms, as gently as if he were lifting his own child.

CHAPTER 8

THE DEVIL'S ANVIL

The thirst-maddened horse stumbled through the new morning into the furnace heat of another noon, its mouth dripping foam, its sunken eyes still fixed with insane hunger on the beaker of water. The wind was rising now, stirring up clouds of choking sand. On the horse's back Max slumped in the saddle, drifting in and out of consciousness as the animal lurched to the top of another salt-crusted dune. The horse staggered once . . . twice . . . and fell to its knees.

Max grunted, jarred out of his stupor by the sudden, sickening vertigo of the motion. He cried out as the animal slowly sagged onto its side, grinding his pinioned leg into the sand as its inert body began to topple over the side of the dune, tumbling and sliding downward. Max's head slammed hard onto the compacted sand, cracking open the clown-faced mask like an eggshell as he was

wrenched and dragged, crushed and half buried in sand
by the falling horses's body. The horse came to rest at
last at the bottom of the dune and lay unmoving.

Max squirmed wildly, frantic with pain and fear, trying to free himself from the dead weight of the dead
animal. He jerked viciously at his bound wrists as panic
gave him new strength, barely feeling the pain in his
hands through the pain of his battered body. The thongs
grated and slid against his slippery skin as fresh blood
soaked them; giving, stretching . . . With a final brutal
wrench his hands pulled free.

Groping blindly, he untied the ropes that had held him
on the horse's back through a day and a half of torture
and dragged his twisted leg out from under its body.
Sitting in the sand, he clawed the suffocating ruin of the
mask from his head and flung it away, taking deep,
gasping breaths of furnace-hot air. He rubbed his swollen
eyes, wiped the sweat from his face, blinking his vision
clear. The sun reflecting from the salt-caked sand was
like sun on metal, blinding him with daggers of light. He
flung up his arm, wincing, shielding his watering eyes
from the glare. The wind whined around him, gusting
harder now; salt and sand stung his raw skin.

Max pushed up onto his knees, opening his eyes more
cautiously this time; searching for the flask of water that
had driven the horse to its death. Raising his head, he
saw the flask lying on its side in the sand, still half full.
The horse lay head-down at the bottom of a dune, its
glassy, sightless eye still fixed on the vision of water.

Max began to crawl over the horse's body toward the
flask, reaching out with a blood-smeared hand. Abruptly,
sickeningly, the horse dropped, sinking beneath his
weight. Max jerked back, startled. He watched in disbe-

lief as the water flask was suddenly swallowed up by the sand, as the horse's head followed. . . .

The sand beneath his own knees began to slide as the horse started to disappear slowly, head-first, into a sinkhole. Max flung himself backward up the slope, his gut knotting with fresh fear as the sand began to suck him down with the sensual hunger of a living thing. Flopping onto his belly, he began to crawl back up the side of the dune. The sand caved in around his legs; the dune wall crumbled, dragging him back and down.

Behind him the entire bottom of the dune collapsed, swallowing more of the horse. Max scrambled desperately, slipped back again, sinking deeper; scrambled higher with the superhuman strength of sheer terror. His legs broke free of the sand; kicking and struggling, he fought his way to the top of the dune. He flung himself onto the crest, looked back just in time to see the horse disappear entirely.

He lay still for a long moment, sobbing with relief, before he found the strength to push himself up again. He peered on over the edge of the dune. A small, inhuman face bobbed up in front of him and screamed, showing rows of white, gleaming teeth. Max screamed, too, recoiling as his ragged nerves betrayed him. Losing his balance, he fell back down the side of the dune.

Frantically he stopped his slide, spread-eagling on the sand; began to scramble up again, his dazed mind realizing too late that it had been his own monkey he had seen up there . . . that as it turned and ran screaming, it had been dragging a water bottle. He hauled himself back to the top of the dune. *Water.* . . .

The monkey was waiting for him. Max almost could have sworn that it looked embarrassed. He jerked the flask from its back, ripping the stopper open. He drank heedlessly, unable to stop himself until he had drained nearly half the bottle. Then, as the monster of his own thirst let him breathe again, he shared a long drink with his parched pet. Restoppering the water bag, he slung it at his shoulder. He lifted the monkey into his arms as he stumbled to his feet, scratching its head in wordless gratitude.

He tucked the monkey carefully into the front of his jacket, stood on the crest of the dune, for the first time getting a good look at what they had both come through . . . what they were facing now. The endless, undulating salt wastes surrounded them on every side, stretching away to every point on the horizon, as if there were nothing else in the world. The gusting wind sand-blasted his exposed skin; it was nearly impossible to keep his eyes open.

His hope withered. Already the windblown sand was covering the horse's meandering tracks, and the monkey's, the only thread he had to lead him out of this deathtrap. But there was no point in standing here like a jackass, watching the rest of the trail disappear like the horse behind him. Ducking his head against the wind, he began to trudge back along the vanishing line of tracks, staggering and sliding in the loose sand.

The trail disappeared completely inside of an hour. The feeble sense of direction that Max had clung to disappeared with it. The wind was no guide: It came from nowhere and everywhere, changing quarters again and again to strike at him from some unprotected angle. He could barely make out the sun through the swirling haze of the rising sandstorm, and he had no idea which way Bartertown lay from here, even if he had been able to follow the sun or the wind home. He kept walking, telling himself that he would find a way out if he only kept moving; because it was the only chance he had left, and he was the only one left who gave a damn whether he did.

The rest of the day passed, and the new night followed; another day and another night . . . and still he saw nothing ahead but what he had seen behind; still he was lost, wandering in circles for all he could tell. By the dawn of the third day Max could barely remember a time beyond this time, a life when he had not stumbled through a blazing inferno, everyexposed bit of his skin raw and blistered, his cracked lips bleeding, and his eyes on fire from windblown salt and sand.

He shared the last trickle of brackish water from the bottle with the whimpering monkey, at what he guessed, uncertainly, was around midday. Then he threw the empty bag away, hating the sight of it now, glad to be rid of even that much weight. Dragging himself to his feet, he started on again, wading through the drifts, and the sand began its endless task of burying, burying the empty water bag, his footprints, any trace at all that any living thing had violated the pristine lifelessness of its surface.

Two more days passed, light and darkness, heat and cold, an endless spinning wheel of time . . . a rack on which a man's body and soul were slowly pulled to pieces. Max no longer had any sense of time, any memory at all. He knew now that he had been slowly choking to death on his own swollen tongue forever . . . that every breath he took had always sent pain shooting through him like a stake driven through his heart, that every stumbling step had always been harder than the last, that the sandstorm would never end. The screaming wind would keep pushing him back with every step forward that he took, until eternity. Somewhere along the way he had died and gone to hell and never even noticed the difference.

He kept on, shambling, crawling, staggering up and on

again, blindly retracing his own steps, his face a salt-
crusted death mask, his eyes fever-haunted. Still he carried the monkey cradled obsessively against his chest—
driven like an animal by a deeper, fiercer, far less rational
thing than hope; the thing that had kept him alive for
twenty long years against all the odds. And even that was
a part of his damnation.

Max staggered up another rise, fell on his face as the
loose sand slid and shifted, jerking his feet out from
under him for the thousandth time. Spitting uselessly, he
tried to push himself up again, his body trembling with
effort. He sagged back as the burning sand reached up
for him with a lover's heat, welcoming him. He struggled
to lift his head, resisting. . . .

A hand exploded through the sand, closed over Max's
face with suffocating ferocity, wrenching him down
again, choking, smothering; sucking him deeper and
deeper into the desert's hidden heart. He tore through a
membrane like a tissue of flesh, as below him more hands
reached up, grabbing, clawing. . . .

Max plunged into nothingness, toward Thunderdome
waiting below, its surface crawling with bodies. Countless hands reached up like writhing snakes, to drag him
back through an endless loop of nightmare, back to its
beginning; to make him relive it over and over. . . .

Max screamed, lunging back and up in a spasm of
horror, bursting back through the membrane—up out of
the burning bed, the velvet pillow of smothering sand—
gasping for air as the delirium dream fell away. He
scrambled to his feet and ran on, stumbling, fleeing in
blind terror from the thing that lay waiting, waiting
beneath the sand.

But waiting was a game of time, and the desert had
eternity; with every footstep it silently reclaimed, Max's

time was running out, his life evaporating with every drop of sweat. Second by second the desert sucked him dry, sucked him deeper into its inescapable hourglass, flowing grain on grain toward oblivion. Max staggered on, glare-blind and burning with fever, his breath coming in rasping sobs. One foot lifted, set down, one more foot lifted, set down. . . . The ground dropped out from under him as he stepped off the edge of a dune and fell, falling endlessly—an insect falling, swallowed by his own screaming mouth, a man falling, swallowed up like an insect by the hungry sands.

The ground rushed eagerly to meet him; Max slammed down onto the hard salt pan at the foot of the dune and lay still at last. The howling wind wailed around him, singing a dirge as it began to cover his motionless form. Grain by grain the sand began to erase him from existence, absorbing him into itself as the desert claimed its lover at last.

The wind died finally, as the day began to die. The evening light lay redly on the mound of sand heaped up over Max's inert body, only his face and one shoulder left unburied now. And in the west, silhouetted by the setting sun, a formless shape danced like a mirage through the shivering waves of heat, drawing closer at a slow, ground-eating trot.

The figure resolved little by little into something vaguely human, bristling with spines. Closer still, it became a clear human form, the form of a tribal hunter dressed in skins with a shock of brown hair plastered down by sweat. Carrying three long spears and burdened down beneath her heavy pack, seventeen-year-old Savannah Nix slowed suddenly, raising her head to sniff the breeze. She squinted quizzically, searching around her, shielding her eyes with her hands; frowned as she spotted the unnatural mound of sand lying up ahead.

Trotting forward again, she circled the burial mound, jerked back in surprise as she found a man's face exposed on its lee side. She stood staring for a long moment, her eyes wide with an almost religious awe, before she crouched down beside him, gently brushing away the sand to reveal more of his head.

She pressed her cheek close to his blistered face, felt him barely breathing . . . still alive. *Of course he was alive.* A wide grin pulled at her cracked lips. *It was Walker. She had found him.*

Quickly she began to dig his unconscious body free of the sand, discovering as she did the small creature lying inside his jacket, equally motionless. She took her nearly empty water bottle from her pack, trickled a small stream carefully into the man's mouth. It dribbled out again; he did not stir. She pulled her pack apart, pulling out skins and thongs; lashed together a makeshift litter. Grunting, she dragged the dead weight of the man's body onto the litter and tied him there, the monkey still inside his coat.

Taking a deep breath, she resettled her pack and leaned down to lift the spear handles of the litter. Throwing her weight against it, she began to drag it on across the desert.

Silently the sand began to erase the signs of her passage, and behind her the wasteland was still once more.

CHAPTER 9

CRACK IN THE EARTH

Savannah traveled on resolutely through the darkness, navigating by the stars as she dragged her precious burden toward home and help; knowing that every moment counted and that she did not dare to stop for rest. She had found Walker, but if she didn't get him back to shelter in time, she had found only his corpse. She had been out on this trek for many days and was weary and hungry; dragging a man's dead weight through the sand was getting more and more difficult.

At last, as dawn broke and the land around her began to brighten, she reached the bottom of a final dune and the last of her strength. She could not haul the litter any farther. Leaving it behind her on the sand, she scrambled up the side of the dune alone, searching the horizon.

A smile flickered across her sweat-streaked face. Still far away but within sight lay the red rock rim of a

canyon, marking the deep fissure eaten into the flatlands
by time and flowing water: Crack in the Earth. Home.

She raised her hands, throwing back her head, and
gave a high, ululating cry. Her cry echoed out across the
vast expanse of sand and rock until it reached the canyon's rim.

At the top of the cliffs a small, dirty, freckled boy
named Finn McKoo crouched on the warm rocks, silently
watching as a frill-necked lizard sunned itself on a stone.
He raised his head, his eyes widening as he heard the
distant echo of her call. Scrambling up, he hung out over
the cliff edge and repeated the cry, sending it on again,
down and down into the valley far below.

Far down in the valley bottom, the tiny moving figures
of his friends/family/tribe hesitated, looking up from
their work as they heard his cry. He could make out
about a dozen of them, boys under the age of ten, girls
under fifteen, the Gatherers of the Tribe, collecting
plants, berries, and firewood along the riverbank in the
coolness of early morning.

Midway down the cliff was Mr. Skyfish, a precocious,
stubborn boy of about ten with thick mud-caked hair that
stood out from his head like wings. Climbing to the roof
of the world with his bird-feathered kite strapped to his
back, he stopped to answer the cry and scrambled faster
up the narrow path that wound to the top of the cliffs. As
he climbed, more cries began to rise from below as more
children started toward the pathway and up.

Below Mr. Skyfish, Anna Goanna, a slim, brown-
haired girl of thirteen or fourteen paused in her hunting,
the snake she had just caught still writhing in her hand.
She hesitated, looking up, then twirled the snake around
her head and cracked it like a whip, breaking its back.
Stuffing the dead snake into her catch bag, she began to

run up the slope, Above her, Mr. Skyfish was climbing higher and higher, already nearing the top of the cliffs, the wailing cries following him up.

On the rim of the canyon, Finn McKoo was racing out across the sand, "Savannah! Savannah!"

Ahead of him now, Savannah's form emerged from the heat haze. He ran faster across the hot sand to fling himself into her arms, hugging her, feeling her own arms tighten lovingly around him.

Raising his head from her shoulder, he looked out over her back. He stiffened as he saw what lay at the bottom of the dune behind her: the body of the most terrifying creature he had ever seen ... something that almost looked human, which made it even worse. He let go of Savannah and began to back away, his eyes wide with fright.

Seeing his expression, Savannah climbed to her feet, pointing at the litter as she burst out, "It's him! I finded him. Savannah Nix finded Walker."

Unimpressed, Finn McKoo turned and bolted. Savannah chased after him, exasperated, shouting, "He's done and come for us, Finn McKoo! This here's the salvage!" She grabbed him, jerking him to a halt. Turning him firmly around, she dragged the squirming boy back down the side of the dune to where Max lay. "We's going home," she insisted, her voice gentling, soothing him now.

Finn stared down at Max in trembling awe, his mouth hanging open. A trickle of pee ran down his left leg and disappeared into the sand as sudden fright and excitement got the better of him. "Tomorrow-morrow-Land?" he murmured.

Savannah nodded eagerly. "Yeah, We's gonna live in a

high-scraper ... we's gonna see the video-o-o ..." The
magical word rolled off her tongue like a yodel.

She kneeled down beside Finn, hugging him close, as
they gazed at Max's face in wonder. "We's found," she
whispered. She glanced up as she heard the distant voices
of the approaching Gatherers. A familiar apparition
soared above the dunes—the bird form of Mr. Skyfish's
kite dancing on the warm updrafts. Then, one by one, the
sun-browned faces and ocher-daubed heads of the Tribe
appeared. Mr. Skyfish trailed behind the others now, his
kite soaring above them like an eagle.

The Gatherers ran toward Savannah, calling out in
welcome, until they saw what lay on the litter beside her.
They slid to a stop, their grins turning to grimaces of
doubt and horror, bumping into each other as they began
to back away again just like Finn McKoo.

Finn, feeling braver now, called out proudly, "It's
Walker. I touchded him."

Mr. Skyfish moved forward, bolder than the rest. "Tell
the balls of it," he demanded.

Savannah got to her feet again, pointing as she glanced
back at the desert behind her. "In the Nothing. Place
where salt meet sand. I's doin' hunter trot 'cos I got thirst
on my back."

The Gatherers, following Mr. Skyfish, began to
approach again slowly.

"Day's running, night's coming," Savannah recited,
her voice falling easily into the cadences of a storyteller.
"But down the pike I gets animal snifter—strong and
sour. Then another. I plays follow me to hump in ground.
Him there. All still. Just waiting."

Mr. Skyfish and the others kneeled down beside Max,
gazing at his face, his battered leather jacket. Mr.
Skyfish reached out, passing his hand over Max's body,

Mel Gibson is Mad Max.

Tina Turner as Aunty Entity.

Master and Blaster come to battle.

Road warrior for hire.

The Thunderdome, arena of the future.

Aunty Entity watches
as Blaster prepares
for battle.

Orphaned children of the desert

The chase is on...

Max plans his next move.

never quite touching the bloody, sun-blistered face or the
sand-caked leather as he stared at the motionless man on
the litter. "She ain't pissing us," he murmured. "It's
him."

The children around him shivered, as if they were
witnessing a holy vision.

Mr. Skyfish looked up at Savannah. "When he do the
flying, he standing up or lying down?" he asked, his eyes
bright with excitement.

Savannah shook her head. "I ain't seen that." She
shrugged. "I told you straight. I finds him in the hump. I
drags him back."

Anna Goanna stepped up beside her. "If it's Walker,
why ain't he flying?" she demanded, always a little
resentful of Savannah's self-important claims and
dreams.

Mr. Skyfish tapped his head with a finger. "Use your
program," he said impatiently. "Or you so wasted, you
ditch your history'n all? What about us? What about the
ol' crash landin'?" He pointed at Max. "He musta got
mugged by the Turbulents. That's why he's all mashed
up."

A five-year-old named Eddie pushed through the
crowd, ignoring the arguments of his elders as he crept to
the side of the mysterious stranger. Reaching out, he
touched Max tentatively.

A brown, fuzzy head popped out of Max's jacket; the
monkey stared in astonishment at the ring of watching
faces.

Eddie fell back in amazement. The children danced
back around him, some of them giving little shrieks of
surprise.

Anna Goanna pointed at the monkey, skepticism plain

on her face. "Okay, schlock-cock," she said to Mr. Skyfish, "who's he?"

Mr. Skyfish put his fists on his hips. "You reckon Walker rides alone? No sir, not on a long track. He packs a buddy." He bent his head at the monkey. "He's worded co-pilot. That's why he's littler and uglier."

Eddie, recovered from his initial fright, crept forward agains, smiling at the monkey. "Walker's ugly," he said. "He ain't." He waved shyly.

Savannah gave an impatient command, and the Gatherers picked up Max's litter. They carried him on across the dunes to the canyon rim, passing through a long, black finger of shadow. Most of them scarcely bothered to glance up, but Savannah did and smiled, her heart filling with pride. Soon they would all have the knowing and the doing again, just as she had always believed.

Carefully they bore the litter down the long, tortuous path that led to the bottom of the canyon. At the quiet river's edge they clambered into the battered, heavily patched life raft that had once been part of an aircraft's survival equipment, some of them straddling the outrigger lashed onto its side for better stability. Loading the litter aboard, they set out downriver, paddling easily through the shadowed water that lay like a green ribbon between the smoothly vertical walls of blood-red sandstone.

At last they reached a small beach cupped in a hollow of the canyon wall. More children of different ages were wading in the water, drawing fishnets in toward shore while others tended camp fires, cleaning and smoking the catch.

As they drifted up to the shore Anna Goanna stood up in the raft, calling out, "Gekko! Gekko! It's Walker. C'mon, ditch the fishes!" She looked toward the place where a dead tree rose from the water at the edge of the shore; sitting on a platform in its fork was her boyfriend Gekko, fishing with a pole, the leg he had injured in a fall propped up beside him, heavily bandaged in bark and rags. On his head he wore a pair of salvaged headphones, connected by bits of wire to a chunk of a plane's instrument panel strapped against his chest. Tied to his back was a forked stick with an old LP wedged onto it, rising above his head like a halo. He looked up at her call, his face filling with sudden excitement.

Beyond him, among the fishers wrestling in their catch, a blond girl of about sixteen named Cusha looked up and dropped her corner of the net. She hurried awkwardly along the sand, slowed only a little by the bulge of an eight-months' pregnancy.

"Rattle your ass!" Anna Goanna shouted at Gekko. "It's him!"

The Fishers gathered around as the raft bearing Max scuffed into the sand. Cusha hugged Savannah, licking her friend's face in greeting.

The Gatherers and Fishers together lifted Max from the raft, bearing him on their shoulders along the beach, between boulders, down a long set of rough steps cut from the sandstone. The river followed them down, cascading in a white, foaming wall toward the shallow rock-strewn pool far below. The narrowing canyon opened out again into the wide valley floor where the Tribe's main camp lay. A score of thatched huts, faded nylon bubble tents, and sleeping platforms lay in the shadow of rustling eucalyptus trees and lichen-encrusted boulders. A large fire burned in an open hearth, sheltered from the weather beneath a soot-blackened overhang of rock. Another twenty Tribe members—nursing mothers, fire keepers, cooks, and children too young to gather food—

were already running forward to greet Savannah and the others.

They laid Max's unconscious body down in the center of the camp and crouched around him, suddenly silent and uncertain. A little 'un touched Max's face cautiously. "Very dirty," she said solemnly. Savannah laughed, and the laughter spread, snapping the Tribe's breathless tension.

"What's his jabber?" Gekko asked.

Anna Goanna shook her head impatiently. "He ain't making' wordstuff."

"It were a long track," Cusha murmured, speaking what was obvious to her eyes. "He must be slogged out."

"Maybe," Gekko said thoughtfully. "Or maybe he's just listening."

A tremor passed through the Tribe; their giggles and murmuring dropped to silence again. Mr. Skyfish leaned close to Max's face. "Walker . . ." he called softly. "Hello, Walker . . ."

The children waited breathlessly. There was no response from the battered figure lying still on the ground.

Mr. Skyfish shrugged, satisfied, having proved that Walker was not listening.

"Maybe he is jabberin'," Gekko insisted. "But we ain't hearing."

Mr. Skyfish waved his hand. "You can see. His licketys ain't movin'."

"Not with wordstuff." Gekko shook his head stubbornly. "With the sonic." He gestured at the bizarre rig he wore.

Mr. Skyfish frowned. "That thing ain't never gonna work," he said scornfully. "Sonic-bonic-bullshit." At least his kite really flew.

But Gekko slipped the headphones over his ears and spun the record on its stick. Holding the record's disc over Max, he twiddled the nobs on his chest. "This here's Delta-Fox-X-ray. Can you hear me? Delta-Fox-X-ray . . . come in, please . . . Anybody out there? . . . Can you read me, Walker?"

The other children tittered nervously, caught somewhere between awe and scorn.

And looking out from the darkness of a cave halfway up the red rock wall, a strange, inhuman-looking face peered down at the children below, all laughing and staring around Max's body. No one down there bothered to look up, knowing that it was only Scrooloose who watched them—the tribe's self-styled shaman, his skin white with ash, his eyes black-ringed with soot, and his dark, half-shaven-off hair standing one end like a cockatoo's crest.

Ecstatic and terrified, Scrooloose turned away and scuttled back into his cave. Wrapping an old airline blanket tightly around his shoulders, he crouched down before the altar he had made, a tiny framework strung with bones and fetishes, surrounded by the skulls of the Tribe's revered ancestors. He reached out with a quivering hand, to touch the hide painting that formed the centerpiece of his altar—the portrait of an airline pilot in peaked cap and uniform jacket. Walker had returned. . . .

CHAPTER 10

THE RETURN OF WALKER

Max lay on a rush mattress on the floor of a sleeping platform high above the ground, jacketless, shirtless, and still unconscious. A canopy of parachute cloth draped the platform's walls and roof, billowing gently in the breeze, protecting him from staring eyes as the tribe kept its vigil below, chanting endlessly, "Walker . . . Walker . . . Walker. . . ."

"Savannah sat at Max's side with a bowl and a pair of ancient scissors. She had already shaved him, and carefully washed the sand and blood from his sun-blistered face. She began to clip his hair short, placing each handful of tangled, sand-filled hair in a bowl beside her."

Across the platform Eddie and a tiny girl named Gus were bathing the ecstatic monkey in a jar, giggling with delight, their own much-loved stuffed toys lying forgotten on the floor. They had already pried off one of Max's

114

boots and painted his toes ocher. As Savannah glanced up with a smile, watching the two little 'uns and the monkey, a hand slipped silently under the edge of the canopy. It grabbed a handful of hair clippings and disappeared again.

Mr. Skyfish climbed down the laddered platform leg, proudly brandishing his prize to the others waiting below. The platform waded in the quiet pool, two legs in the water and two on land. Other children clung to the posts, trying to get a glimpse of Max.

As Mr. Skyfish reached the ground he began to pass out locks of hair. Nearly the entire Tribe was gathered below Walker's resting place now, gazing up; only Cusha, preoccupied these days with the life growing inside her, had waded on into the pond to pour water over her distended belly, singing softly to her unborn baby. Some of the others had gathered together bundles of their possessions, ready for a journey. At the water's edge Anna Goanna bathed Gekko's infected leg with gentle care.

The day passed on into darkness; the full moon rose, peeping down between the cliffs at the village below as midnight came and went. Torchlight flung the eerie shadows of the watchers high up the red stone walls as their chanting droned on. Some of the children had given up and gone to sleep by now, either creeping back to their own platforms or lying down in the open where they were.

Savannah still kept her weary vigil, sitting with Walker's head cradled in her lap. The little 'uns had painted his face ocher; she had let them, because red was the color of life. He still had not awakened or shown any sign of life beyond just breathing. Sipping water from a gourd, she leaned over him as she had done many times during the day, pried his jaw open, and let the water trickle with infinite care from her mouth into his own. His throat worked spasmodically, instinctively swallowing; this time he made a small sound, not even a whimper, as the water went down. That was a good sign . . . anything was. She sighed, glancing away at the two little 'uns curled up with the monkey against Walker's side, all of them sleeping soundly. She rubbed her own eyes and moved along Max's body to his foot. Taking a length of rope, she knotted it around his ankle, tying him securely to the platform as the Tribe tied down all their captive birds. She couldn't take the chance that he might wake in the night and fly away without them.

Satisfied, she curled up along his other side, resting her head on his shoulder, and let herself drift down into sleep at last. It had been a long day but tomorrow would be a better one. . . .

The ladybug crept laboriously along the hollow surface of Max's cheek, as oblivious as if it had been climbing the side of a sand dune, bound for some more satisfactory destination. Abruptly the earth beneath the ladybug began to undulate; Max's jaw twitched. Max stirred for the first time since he had lost consciousness almost two days before. The light of a new morning filtered through the canopy, touching his eyelids with a gentle finger. Wild birds twittered, waking in the trees, and on the peak of the platform roof the Tribe's captive birds answered; the sound of chanting had stopped altogether somewhere during the night. Max sighed as the blackness where his mind had lain buried slowly gave way to the peaceful shadowland of normal sleep.

Two terminally curious ten-year-old girls climbed up over the rear of the sleeping platform, stifling their nervous giggles as they slipped beneath the canopy's edge. Savannah and the little 'uns lay sound asleep alongside Max, oblivious to the intruders creeping toward him. Moving up past his feet, they crouched down by his waist; a small hand reached tentatively toward his fly and yanked.

Max's eyes bulged open as alarms went off in his subconscious. He sat bolt upright, staring, scattering sleeping bodies right and left. The two girls screamed, the monkey screeched; Savannah and the little 'uns cried out in astonishment and fright. Half awake and surrounded by screaming strangers, Max screamed too. His body was already on its knees, reacting by pure instinct, scrambling backward. . . .

Before they could reach him, he had backed through the canopy and off the edge of the platform. Losing his balance with a cry, he fell out and down . . . was jerked up short midway between the earth and sky as the rope around his ankle stopped his plunge. He dangled upside down, swinging through a sickening arc, the floor of the platform above him, the shining pool below. Topsy-turvy, he stared at the mass of small faces streaming past below/above him, shouting their delight.

Struggling awkwardly, he managed to catch hold of his own leg; he jackknifed himself upright with gasping effort, focusing his eyes on the platform he had fallen from. More faces gaped down at him. A handful of birds, pinioned by the foot like he was, fluttered into the sky, squawking in distress.

A boy with a kite tied to his back clambered up one of the laddered posts beside him, brandishing a knife. The boy began to hack through the rope while Max watched in dizzy disbelief, shouting, "Fly, Walker! Fly!"

The rope snapped in two, and Max plunged helplessly into the pond as the children below scattered, screaming.

Max floundered facedown in the water, his eyes wide-open, barely able to remember to hold his breath. The water was scarcely two feet deep; below his face he saw the rocky bottom of the pond with startling clarity. Max pushed himself up, sitting back, shaking his dripping head; wide-awake now but too dazed to believe anything that had happened, that he was actually sitting up to his chest in water, in a valley filled with green trees and huts . . . all alone. The children he was sure he had seen a moment ago had disappeared. Any minute he would wake up, spitting sand, still dying in the desert.

He got to his knees, struggled to his feet. "Whoa!" His trembling legs betrayed him and he fell backward, splashing down again hard in the water.

"Whoa . . . whoa . . . whoa!" His cry echoed around him in the high-pitched tones of children's voices.

"Whoa!" The sound came down from above; he looked up, bewildered, just in time to see faces up on the platform, before they ducked back inside the tent. They *were* real . . . just in hiding. Somebody had found him . . . he was alive. He was actually sitting up to his chest in water.

He fell forward onto his hands, supporting himself with one shaky arm while his free hand pulled water up to his mouth, shoveling it down his tortured throat; he drank and drank with mindless gratitude, sure there would never be enough to stop his thirst. As his sanity and senses slowly came back to him, his ears began to register echoes again. He glanced up, looking around. Some of the hidden children were emerging from behind rocks and trees, creeping cautiously toward him . . . slurping. Mimicking his every sound.

He turned where he sat as reason and curiousity got

firmer footing in his brain, and saw a basket of fruit hanging from one of the sleeping platforms. Never taking his eyes off the children, he climbed to his feet again, more carefully this time, and rebuttoned his pants. Then, slowly, he began to back out of the pond toward the fruit, one uncertain step at a time.

The children seemed to be of all ages, dressed in hides, their hair plastered with red and yellow mud. They separated around him and then closed in again as he passed, grinning fatuously. He glanced back at the basket of fruit, started as he saw his monkey suddenly drop down off the platform into the basket; it began to peel a banana, chattering happily at the sight of him. Relieved and somehow reassured by the monkey's presence, Max grabbed a piece of fruit and choked it down, hardly taking the time to chew.

A small hand tugged at his dripping T-shirt, held up another fruit as he finished the first. He took it, gulping it down, eating like there was no tomorrow. His stomach began to hurt, but he welcomed a bellyache, anything that proved he was really alive again.

Savannah climbed down from the sleeping platform, starting toward Max as children bounded past her, carrying more fruit. Other Tribe members, seeing that Walker wanted food, ran every which way around her, competing for offerings to lay before him.

The children began to crowd around Max again, holding out an offering or starting to eat it themselves. They wolfed the food down as if they were starving, still imitating his every move.

Unnerved, Max began to back away from them again, wading through the water, still eating. They followed, gazing up at him almost worshipfully. He looked from side to side, studying their grimy faces. They really were all children, none of them out of their teens, most of them much younger. Where were the adults? And why in God's name were they staring at him like that? "Who are you?" he said at last. The sound of his own voice startled him.

"Who are you?" The Tribe repeated the words, the sound rippling through them.

"What the hell ..." he muttered, half under his breath; unease crawled up his spine.

The children repeated it very softly.

More clearly Max asked, "Who brought me?"

Louder, they repeated every word.

"Your parents?" Max insisted, raising his voice. "Where are they?"

Even louder, they shouted it back at him.

"Answer me!" Max ordered angrily.

"Answer me!" the Tribe yelled back, their eyes wide with feverish excitement, crowding in as he tried to back away again.

"Shut up!" Max bellowed, furious with panic and exasperation.

The Tribe screamed the words.

Still backing away, Max put his fingers into his mouth and whistled shrilly. A score of whistles echoed back at him, shattering his nerves. The children had driven him into the center of the camp now; Max stood near the fire pit, at his wits' end, his hands over his ears.

Something heavy plummeted down into the mob of children from somewhere up above, landing squarely at Max's feet. The children leaped back in surprise.

Max looked down, found a bloody, severed boar's head lying in front of him. Around him the Tribe were turning, looking up. Max looked up, too, and saw a boy of about eighteen standing on a ledge high above them. He stood

with the proud confidence of a warrior, his hair clotted
with ocher, and wearing the trophies of past hunts—
necklaces of animal teeth and bones—a loincloth, and
not much else. In his hand he held a rifle with a spear
lashed to its barrel. He was Slake M'Thirst, the Tribe's
chief Hunter and nominal leader. Strung out behind him
were eight other teenage boys, all Hunters. Between
them, slung from a spear, they carried the body of a wild
boar. They all stared down at the gathering below, their
eyes riveted on Max.

Never taking his eyes off the stranger, Slake hurled his
spear in a blur of sudden motion. It impaled itself in the
eye of the boar's head, dead on-target, a testimony and a
threat.

Savannah moved quickly and protectively to Max's
side, calling out, "We's found, Slake...."

Slake caught hold of the long rope suspended from the
rocks above him, stretching across above their heads to
the far wall of the canyon. Dangling from a strip of hide,
he slid down the rope, dropped off at its center, landing
on a rocky ledge just above the crowd. He stared again at
Max, leaped down, and waded slowly through the Tribe.
The other Hunters began to climb down the cliff, excited
but more cautious.

The children stepped back as Slake drew closer to
Max. Slake prowled around the stranger in a half crouch,
moving as cautiously as a cat, his hands out as if he were
sensing the older man's aura. He jerked back suddenly,
eyes wide, sucking in his breath.

The Tribe mimicked the sound.

"Who are you?" Max asked.

The Tribe repeated it.

Slake threw out his arms, commanding silence. "We's
the waiting ones," he said, his eyes fixed on Max's face.

Max hesitated, uncertain. He was going to have to take this slow. Carefully he asked, "Waiting for what?"

"Waiting for you," Slake murmured, his voice full of awe.

The words *for you* echoed softly through the Tribe.

Max flung up his arms, hands out, repeating Slake's gesture for silence. "Is this all of you?"

Slake nodded. "Now we counts fifty-two."

"Where are your parents?" Max asked again, this time hoping he might really get an answer.

But Slake and Savannah only looked at each other, their faces blank. Slake shook his head. "Ain't got that code, Walker. What's parents?"

Max shifted nervously as the unease that had been with him ever since he woke up crawled farther up his spine. They called him Walker. They thought he was somebody he wasn't. They might only be children, but there were a lot of them, and they were armed with stone axes and spears and knives . . . . The best thing he could think of to do now was to play along until he understood things better. "Who . . . gave birth to you?" he asked, trying to think of a way to make the question clearer.

Slake shrugged. "We birthed ourselves," he said. Turning, he pointed at a fuzzy-headed toddler standing nearby. "He be Cusha's first. Savannah popped Little Finn." He gestured at the tall girl beside him.

"Yeah." Max nodded encouragingly. "But who birthed *you*?"

A puzzled murmur spread through the Tribe. Slake stared at Max in open surprise, as if he should somehow already have known. "Her name were Joanna. 'Member her? She were a fire keeper." He raised his eyebrows.

"Yeah," Max answered uncertainly. "Well, where is she now?"

Slake waved his arm, gesturing vaguely at infinity. "Her time come. She took the leaving."

Max frowned. "She died?"

The children's faces changed, registering confusion and fright.

"No," Slake said emphatically, shaking his head. "She took the leaving." His own face filled with distress and incomprehension. He looked hard at Savannah. The Tribe's confusion was turning to panic now as the word *died* rippled through them.

"She were one of a count of eight," Savannah said with peculiar urgency, as if she were trying to jog Max's memory. "I 'member 'em . . . trotting way out till you couldn't sight 'em no more." She swept the cliffs with her own hand. "All night long we sang 'em a chant for luck."

"Oh, yeah," Max murmured, nodding, realizing how closely he had brushed disaster, "uh-huh, right." Christ, he could hardly remember his own name right now, let alone figure out what the hell they wanted from him.

"What you wordin', Walker?" Slake asked anxiously. "They didn't find you?"

Max backed up another step, unable to control his desperate urge to get away from this surreal inquisition. "I don't know," he said awkwardly. "You meet a lot of people out there. . . ."

The Tribe looked at one another again, more puzzled now than distressed. Their voices rose and mingled. "What's his program? How come he didn't know? What's happened to his 'memberment? It were history back. Don't he know his own tell?"

The kid with the kite on his back sidled up to Slake, whispering. "I reckon he's testin' us?"

Slake's face brightened; he turned back to Max. "This

a testin', Captain?" he asked earnestly. "You reckon we been slack?"

Max bit his lip. "I dunno," he mumbled, "maybe. . . ."

"We ain't." Slake shook his head. "We kept it straight. Everything marked, everything 'membered, you'll see." Slake moved past Max and away through the children to a small hollow eaten out of the cliff wall. Sitting beneath the shelter was a wooden frame with a bell-shaped piece of airplane fuselage strung below it like a gong. Wind chimes dangled from hide strips around it; with a start Max realized that they were cartridges from a high-powered rifle. Slake picked up a hide-wrapped ax and struck the bell hard. The loud *bong* echoed out across the village and away down the canyon, announcing to the Tribe and the desert beyond that the time had come for another Tell.

CHAPTER 11

THE TELL

For the rest of the day the Tribe allowed Max the
freedom to eat and sleep, recovering his strength and
gathering his wits for the coming evening's performance,
which he hoped would finally explain everything. He had
seen a lot of strange things in his years in the desert but
none of them stranger than this.

Dusk came early to the canyon bottom. As darkness
fell the Tribe reassembled before a stretch of the sheer
canyon wall, sitting cross-legged in a circle of blazing
torchlight. The pungent smell of wood smoke and eucalyptus rose into the cooling air as they settled down,
decked out in their best possessions—a bizarre assortment of metal, fur, and odd relics of civilization dangling
from their necks, wrists, and clothing. Max sat in a place
of honor—the dusty ruins of an airplane seat—in the
middle of the sea of waiting children. The girl who had

found him in the desert sat beside him, gazing up at him with an expession that made him uncomfortable. Her close-cropped brown hair and intense, sharp-featured face were framed by a headdress of furs. The two little 'uns nestled like hounds at his feet; Gus sucked her thumb with a loud, slurping noise while Eddie hugged his teddy bear close on his lap. Max looked down at them in silent incredulity, their contented presence somehow more unreal than anything that had happened to him so far.

Slake stepped out of the shadows into the torchlight, his face stained red with ocher. Gekko and Mr. Skyfish held up torches beside him, illuminating his painted face with a surreal, flickering light. Slake held a small slide viewer in one hand, and the Telling Stick in the other—a handle topped by a rectangular frame dangling with fetishes and feathers. He held the box frame up in front of his face, transforming himself into a demon commentator on some hellish version of the evening news.

"This you knows," he said somberly, his tenor voice ringing out across the hushed sea of faces. The children sat staring at the hide screen that obscured the wall behind him, like the crowd waiting for a Saturday matinee. "I be First Tracker and times past count I done the Tell. But it weren't me that tumbled Captain Walker. It were Savannah. It only right she take the Tell."

The Tribe murmured its approval as Savannah rose from her place at Max's side and moved forward to stand beside Slake. Turning to face the others, she accepted the Telling Stick from his hand and called out in a strong, vibrant voice, "This ain't one body's tell. It's the Tell of us all. We got it mouth to mouth, so you gotta lissen it and 'member—'cos what you hears today, you gotta tell the birthed tomorrow. . . ."

Around Max the young Hunters who stood holding firebrands began to douse their flames. One of the children offered him a bowl filled with what looked like extremely burned popcorn. He took a handful dubiously, flipped one into his mouth and chewed . . . roasted berries. He ate the rest, pleased and somewhat relieved.

Gekko and Mr. Skyfish moved to the screen behind Savannah. "I's lookin' behind us now," Savannah murmured, "across the count of time." She turned, watching as they drew aside the screen. "Down the long haul . . . into history and back." She raised her hand. On the wall behind her was a series of crude paintings and carvings.

The Tribe began to make a loud, shrill whistling sound that made the hair stand up on the back of Max's neck: the sound of a bomb falling.

Savannah raised the Telling Stick. "I sees the end what were the start." She pointed with the Stick to the first image on the Wall, framing a mushroom cloud, the earth and sky around it littered with stick-figure bodies. "It's the Pox-Eclipse, full of pain. . . ."

Max looked around him in bewildered surprise as the children became a writhing mass, moaning and screaming, their faces contorted with anguish, some of them mimicking the sound of a bomb exploding; acting out the events they were being shown on the Wall.

Savannah's voice rose above the storm of sound. "And out of it were birthed cracklin' dust and fearsome time." The Tribe made the sound of a desolate wind howling. "It were full on winter, and Mr. Dead trackin' 'em all. But there were one he couldn't catch." The Hunters began a primitive, guttural moan; the girls counterpointed with a high-pitched, haunted trilling. "That were Captain Walker," Savannah said proudly, and Max felt faces turn to stare at him. "He gathers up a gang, catches the wind, and rides the sky." She pointed the Telling Stick at the second painting on the wall: a crude profile of a 747, peppered with tiny marks that Max realized were meant to represent passengers. Around him the children rustled and settled into new positions, forming themselves into ranks like rows of seats, humming and swinging bullroarers as they made the sound of engines.

"So they ditch the homeland," Savannah recited, "said bidey-bye to the high-scrapers . . ." The children waved farewell to civilization with happy grins. "And what were left of the knowing they left behind." She turned back to the Wall. "Some say the wind just stoppered, others reckon it were a gang called Turbulents." She moved the Telling Stick to the third main image: a 747 on the ground, its back broken, crosses scattered over its frame and the earth . . . a body count. The sputtering and coughing of an engine dying filled Max's ears along with the words; now it became a high-pitched whine and the sound of a crash. The children thrashed on the ground, crawling out of imaginary wreckage.

"And when it were quiet," Savannah went on, more softly, as silence fell, "some had been jumped by Mr. Dead, and some had got the luck. And it leads 'em here. . . ." She turned away from the Wall, the tragic mask of her face transforming with the joy of discovery. She raised her hands, looked up at the sky, embracing the oasis and their new world. "One look and they's got the hots for it. They word it—from that rock to them woods"—sweeping her hands across the canyon—"planet 'Erf. And they says: 'We don't need the knowin', we can live here.'"

The Tribe repeated the words reverently. On the ledge before his shrine Scrooloose watched the Tell with the monkey sitting beside him, munching berries as he silently mouthed the words with the rest: "We don't need the knowin', we can live here."

Mr. Skyfish and Gekko began to beat out a rhythm with sticks, marking the passage of time, as Savannah pointed to a wide bank of dating marks etched into the Wall. "Time counts, and keeps counting . . . and some of 'em gets to missing what they had. They gets sore lonely for the high-scrapers and the v-v-video."

'V-v-v-video-o-o-o," the children crooned, a paean of longing.

"And they does the showin' so the others will 'member what it were like." Savannah brandished the Telling Stick.

"It were the number-one blockbuster telling," Mr. Skyfish cried.

"In stereo-o-o-o-sonic," Gekko chimed in.

Slake came back to Savannah's side, holding the slide viewer. Flanked by Mr. Skyfish and Gekko, they moved through the crowd toward Max. Slake offered him the viewing box; Max took it dutifully and raised it to his eyes. Slake pushed in a faded slide.

Max blinked his eyes into focus, saw a smudged, dust-blurred image of a city's skyline at night, the lights of a bridge arcing across the darkened harbor.

Savannah intoned, "They say: 'Member this?"

"Tomorrow-morrow-Land," the Hunters responded in chorus. "The Knowin' and the doin' of it all." The rest of the Tribe picked up the new refrain; one of the children scrambled to his feet and began to dance as they chanted, "The Knowin' and the doin' and the doin' and the knowin' and the knowin' and the doin' . . ." Max lowered the viewer, looking around him.

As the chanting droned on a second image was pushed

into the viewer. Max lifted it to his eyes again. Another
image of the City at Night—freeways flowing by, trailing
time-lapse ribbons of brilliant scarlet and silver car-
lights. "'Member this?" Savannah cried.

"The River of Light," the Hunters responded.

A third slide: A sunset shot of a jumbo jet flying over
the city.

"'Member this?"

"Skyraft!" the Hunters shouted.

Another slide. "'Member this?" The picture of an
airline pilot gazing skyward as two jets flew overhead.

"Captain Walker!" the Tribe cried. They all turned to
look at Max again.

Max kept his eyes glued to the viewer as the pilot's
picture was removed and another one dropped in.

"'Member this?"

Max recoiled in surprise as the image of a nightclub
stripper suddenly appeared in front of his eyes.

"Mrs. Walker!" the children screamed ecstatically.

Max lowered the viewer, looking around him again as
the Hunters began to beat out a new rhythm, thumping
their spear butts on the stone, a heavier, more ominous
sound. The children fell silent again, their faces no longer
smiling.

Savannah, with Gekko and Mr. Skyfish at her sides,
moved back to the Wall and raised her Telling Stick
again. "So's Captain Walker picked them of an age and
good for a long haul. They counted twenty and that were
them. The First Leaving." She pointed her Telling Stick
at the Wall again, framed the painfully etched words:
RESCUE PARTY, DEPARTED ON THE 8.11.05. LED BY FLIGHT
CAPTAIN G. L. WALKER. Beneath it were nineteen names
also scratched into the Wall, but not deeply enough. Like
the date, they were already becoming difficult to read as

erosion of the soft stone erased their scarring grain by grain. More deeply etched below, so that Max could read them easily, were the words: MAY GOD HAVE MERCY ON OUR SOULS.

Savannah looked out at the watchers. "They said bidey-bye to them what they birthed. And from out of the nothing they looked back, and Captain Walker hollered: 'Wait. One of us will come.'"

"One of us will come," the Tribe murmured.

Savannah's eyes darkened. "But nobody come. So's them of an age took their own leaving. That be the Second." She pointed to a second set of etchings, more primitive than the first, no names but a clutch of clothespin figures and calendar scratches, decorated with writhing snakes and totem creatures.

"Wait," the children droned. "One of us will come. . . ."

"And then be the Third." Savannah showed them the markings of the Third Leaving, fewer figures, more primitive still, marked with childish sun-figures and things that looked like bugs.

"Wait," the children murmured mournfully. "One of us will come. . . ."

Savannah took a deep breath. "And then come the Fourth." She framed the last drawing, of a solitary woman's figure.

"Savannah Nix," Cusha cried out proudly from somewhere behind Max. "It were her time."

The Tribe picked up the name and began to chant it. Slake flung up his arm impatiently, gesturing for silence.

"And somebody did come." Savannah's voice rose triumphantly. She motioned to a smiling, paint-smeared little boy sitting quietly near the front of the crowd: Scratch, the Tribe's artist. He hesitated, suddenly overcome with shyness as she beckoned him to her side. His friends pushed him up and out, until he went forward to join Savannah. Once up there, his pride took over, and he pushed the screen aside to reveal the final painting.

Max stared at the Wall, stunned, as all around him the children looked up at his face again. On the Wall was unmistakably a painting of him, larger than life-size, scar and all, with arms outstretched like Christ on the cross . . . or the wings of an airplane. On his outstretched arms and shoulders were scores of tiny figures waiting to be borne away: the children of Crack in the Earth, perched on the back of their Savior.

Slake reached up with a stick to remove something that had been hung on the Wall just above the painting's head. Max recognized the remains of a peaked airline pilot's cap, decorated with the remains of a dead bird.

Slake approached Max again, bearing the cap reverently in his hands, Savannah following at his side. Max sat motionless and rigid as Slake set the cap carefully on his head.

"We's heartful to you, Captain Walker," Savannah said, her voice choked with emotion.

"We's ready now," Slake murmured, his eyes bright. "Take us home."

High above, Scrooloose looked on, his own eyes spilling tears, the tears running down his cheeks and smearing tracks in his face paint.

Max sat staring at the painting on the Wall for another long moment, trying to untangle the painful knot of his own emotions. Then, slowly, he got to his feet. Lifting his hand to his head, he took off the cap and dropped it on the chair seat.

The children's faces fell; they gasped and murmured with disbelief.

Slake's ocher-stained face pinched with dismay. "We kept it straight," he said desperately. "It's all there, ain't it? Everything marked, everything 'membered." Suddenly he looked very young, very lost.

"Yeah," Max said, his own voice catching in his throat. He nodded once, not meeting anyone's eyes. "You kept it good. You ain't been slack."

Gekko picked the cap up again and pushed it back into Max's hands. "What we waitin' for?" he cried anxiously.

Max pushed the hat away again. He turned his back on the painting. "That ain't me," he said roughly. "You've got the wrong guy."

Mr. Skyfish tugged at his arm. "Quit joshin', Captain," he said.

"Catch us the wind," Gekko cried.

"We gotta see Tomorrow-morrow-Land!" Anna Goanna called.

The rest of the Tribe started to call out the words, "Home! Home! Tomorrow-morrow-Land."

Max turned back, his hands balled into fists. "Listen!" he said, silencing them. "Right now—let's get two things straight. One—I'm not that man." He pointed at the Wall. "Two—we ain't goin' nowhere."

A dozen voices answered him at once, protesting, calling out questions, close to panic now.

"The knowin'," Cusha cried. "How we gonna get the knowin'?"

"We's gonna ride the sky, ain't we?" Mr. Skyfish asked, pulling at Max's arm again.

"But what about the sonic?" Gekko thumped the equipment on his chest.

"There ain't no sonic," Max snapped.

"See, I told ya," Mr. Skyfish said, turning on Gekko with invidious spite.

"Or flying," Max said bitterly, looking down at Mr. Skyfish. "That's all finished." He slashed the air with his hand.

Mr. Skyfish frowned. "Frogshit!" he yelled. "I's seen it." He gathered up the slides and threw them at Max, pushing his lower lip out. "What about this?"

All around him the Tribe began the slide-viewing chant again, pushing closer around Max.

"'Member this?"

"Tomorrow-morrow-Land: They got the knowing and the doing of it all."

The Hunters began to beat out the heavy rhythm with their spears as the high-pitched voices blurred into a cacophony of defiance: "'Member this? The River of Light! 'Member this? Sky Raft! 'Member this? Captain Walker! 'Member this? Mrs. Walker! The knowing and the doing . . ."

They were all around him now, shouting him down as he tried to answer, the furious pandemonium ringing in his head until it made him giddy.

"Lissen him!" Slake shouted suddenly, lifting his hands, his eyes burning.

The voices fell away into blessed silence.

Slowly Max leaned down, picking up the slide of city lights. He stared at it for a long moment, closed his eyes. He took a deep breath, looking out at the intent, waiting faces again. "There were places like these," he said at last. "They were called cities . . . lots of 'em."

The children's eyes widened with fascination and wonder. Gazing down at them, he felt a dark wonder stir in his own soul. They were all so young . . . Suddenly, looking down at them, he felt old. The world that he had been born into, the civilization he had always believed was forever, indestructible, was gone. None of them had even been alive while it still existed; already it was only a mirage, a legend, a dream to them. He was a dinosaur, one of a dying breed, his world vanished and his fate extinction.

He stood staring down into the eyes of the future; shook his head, forcing himself to go on with what he had been trying to say, pushing the painful words out. "And they had the high-scrapers and the video. And the sonic." He glanced at Gekko. "You got it right—they had the knowin' and the doin' of lots of things." His throat closed and he forced himself to swallow, turned to point at the Wall again, at the mushroom cloud. "Then this happened." He looked back at them, lifting his hands helplessly. "It just ain't there no more."

He leaned down to pick up the cap again, turning it in his hands. Looking up, he said fiercely, "You gotta understand. *This* is home. There ain't nobody coming! There ain't no Captain Walker." He flung the cap away over their heads.

The cap spun away like a Frisbee, arcing across the canyon, and suddenly began to rise again, as if it had taken on a life of its own. It soared skyward as the rising breeze lofted it higher and higher through the trees. As Max stood, watching its flight incredulously, the freshening breeze began to gather strength, setting wind chimes to tinkling all around the camp. The bullets strung around the summoning gong began to clang against its sides. Inside Scrooloose's hidden shrine, even the bones and fetishes began to rattle on their thongs.

The Tribe watched breathlessly as Mr. Skyfish's kite lifted from its wooden cradle, rising into the trees. Mr. Skyfish ran toward it, swinging his bullroarer, sending the deep, thrumming whine into the wind. "This is it!" he shouted.

The rest of the Tribe began to run after him, pouring away down the canyon like a flood in pursuit of the hat, leaving Max abruptly alone. He heard the voice of the wind moaning through the canyons and hollows of the rock, growing stronger and stronger; it pushed against his back like insistent hands.

Scrooloose dropped down from a ledge near Max's side. Max jerked around, startled, as the wild-faced boy touched him fleetingly and then ran on after the others. Max stayed motionless and uncomprehending where he was. Savannah stopped, turning back to look at him from the base of the distant steps, as if she were waiting for something. Gus and Eddie ran back to him, seizing his hands as he still did not move, dragging him forward. He let himself be led, his curiosity overcoming his reluctance. The wind was whipping the treetops wildly now, swirling dust up in clouds as the Tribe raced up the steps and out of the canyon bottom. Savannah started on after the others as she saw Max following; she looked back again and again, reassuring herself that he was still coming as she climbed.

Savannah stopped again when she reached the top of the gorge, waiting impatiently for Max and the little'uns. As Gus and Eddie scrambled up over the brink, Savannah reached out to them, helping Gus over the rim with a tug and a brief smile. Max stumbled into view, still dragged by Eddie, who let go of him at last and ran on ahead.

Max stopped, breathing hard, his ribs aching, his body still shaky from his ordeal in the desert. He looked out across the plain, his eyes following the running herd of children. His jaw dropped as he saw at last what they were running toward.

Lying out on the desert, gleaming in the late sun, was

the monstrous hulk of a 747. It must have hit nose-first, trying for an emergency landing; its cockpit and most of the fuselage were buried in sand. But its gigantic tail section still jutted majestically out of the dunes, a fallen monument to a lost civilization. The sheer size of it filled him with awe. *He had forgotten, he had really forgotten what they could do. . . .*

All of the Tribe were streaming toward it, even crippled Gekko, helped along by Anna Goanna, and Savannah, bringing up the rear—all bent against the wind and running as hard as they could. Max followed at a limping walk, floundering up the last steep side of the dune with an effort of will. Christ, he *was* getting old. He stopped again at last as he reached the dune's crest, staring, his amazement redoubled.

Almost the entire Tribe perched on the spine of the 747's tail section, hunched against the wind. Several of the hunters, led by Slake, were whirling bullroarers now. The throbbing drone of sound merged with the wind in a mournful elegy. Only Savannah and Mr. Skyfish were still moving, walking out along the shining metal of the tail to take their positions.

"Everybody loaded, Captain," Savannah called as she saw him top the rise.

"We got the wind up our ass, Captain," Mr. Skyfish shouted. 'Let's go!"

Max stood on the windswept dune, looking up at the waiting children for another long moment, the dirge droning in his ears. And then he turned his back on them and walked away.

Savannah stared after him, her fur headdress whipping around her face, her dark eyes filling with bewildered disillusionment.

CHAPTER 12

THE LEAVING

It was a glorious morning. Max stretched and yawned, squinted out through the hangings of the sleeping platform at Eden. He had slept like the dead since shortly after he got back to camp. The sun was high in the sky by the time he woke again, its light and heat pouring down between the blood-red cliffs like honey. But as he looked out at the new day the camp around him was empty and silent. Birds twittered in the trees, the only sign of life anywhere. He got up and climbed stiffly down the ladder. The kids were gone; even his monkey was nowhere in sight. He wondered if they were still sitting up there on that goddamned wreck, waiting for him to make it fly. Max helped himself to fruit, resolutely refusing to worry, or even think, about it. They'd have to come down sometime.

He splashed his face with water from the pool and

drank, noticed Gekko's fishing pole lying in the sand. Sitting down on the shore, he picked it up and cast the line out into the blue-green water. The sun warmed his back, baking the stiffness out of his abused muscles and joints; a friend to him now, no longer an enemy, here in this beautiful oasis of peace and plenty. The kids were crazy to want to leave Crack in the Earth; but then, they didn't know what he knew about the world outside it. God willing, they'd never find out. This was a place to spend forever in; a place to grow old in. He sighed with rare contentment, running his hand through his newly cropped hair, and began to hum a gentle, aimless tune.

A hand pushed in front of his face, snatched the fishing pole from his grasp. Gekko hobbled away, frowning, reclaiming his property indignantly.

Max looked up in mild surprise, lulled by the soothing silence until he had almost forgotton that he was not the only human being in the world. The rocks and cliffs above the camp were lined with the Tribe's returning members, their mournful, dirty faces staring down at him, forlorn with betrayal.

Max leaned back, closing his eyes with a smile, stretching out in the sun like a satisfied cat.

The resounding *clang* of a gong startled him back into a sitting position, destroying his reverie once and for all. He turned, looking over his shoulder.

Savannah stood beside the camp gong with Cusha, Finn McKoo, and Mr. Skyfish gathered sullenly around her. The Tribe turned with him to stare at her.

"Who's comin'?" Savannah demanded, her brown eyes flashing a challenge. "We's pullin' on a leavin'."

Slake leaped down from the ledge above her to stand face-to-face, confronting the small group of rebels who had challenged the unity of the band. The other children slowly began to filter down into the canyon bottom, gathering around him.

Max turned away again and settled back comfortably against the rocks with his hands behind his head. It was their problem, and it was as meaningless as their pathetic cargo-cult dreams of rescue. Let them work it out among themselves; they weren't going anywhere.

"There ain't gonna be no leavings," Slake said angrily. "All that stuff's just jerkin' time."

Cusha shook her head, frowning, like they all were. "We work it different."

"We got the trick of it," Savannah said stubbornly.

"Ain't you seen nothin'?" Slake shouted, waving his hand toward Max. "He couldn't catch the wind. There weren't no skyrafting. There ain't gonna be no salvage. This here's our Tomorrow-morrow-Land. He's proof of that."

"Program!" Savannah snapped, cutting him off. Turning to the Tribe, she cried, "All of you program!" She flung out her own arm, pointing to Max. "If he ain't Captain Walker, who is he?"

A murmur of questions and ideas rippled through the Tribe. Max's muscles tensed suddenly as he began to realize where her train of thought was heading.

"He ain't no different to us," she finished, "that's who. So he musta slogged it out on foot."

Max frowned. The goddamn brat was as smart as she was stubborn . . . too smart for her own good.

"She's right, Slake!" Gekko cried. "If he can get here, we can get back." He pushed off from the rock where he was sitting and began to hobble toward the group gathered around Savannah.

Anna Goanna scrambled after him, grabbing his arm, holding him back with fierce possessiveness.

"He ain't much bigger than us, Slake," Mr. Skyfish said, looking at Max again.

Gekko pointed at the monkey, perched in a tree with a banana in its paw, watching the strange ways of humans with silent curiosity. "He did it!" Gekko crowed. "And he's littler."

Savannah nodded. "That's the trick of it." She beckoned with her hand. "Who's comin'?"

About half a dozen more Tribe members, all middle 'uns, began to drift toward Savannah. Gekko broke free of Anna Goanna's grasp and limped away to join them.

"Across the Nothin'!" Anna Goanna shouted after him. "Don't you remember?" Looking at Savannah, she said angrily, "When you found him, weren't he damn near jumped by Mr. Dead?" She jerked her head at Max.

Three of the middle 'uns, hearing her words and suddenly remembering what Max had looked like when he arrived, turned around abruptly and scurried back to stand by Slake.

"Nobody's sayin' it ain't a hard slog." Savannah insisted. "We knows that now. But if we wants the knowin' and the doin', there ain't no easy ride." She put her hands on her hips.

"There ain't no knowin' or doin'," Slake said, his voice sharp with the pain of his own hard acceptance. He was the oldest; he still remembered the despair and the loss of the Elders. "There ain't no sonic, there ain't no skyrafting." He glared a the two younger boys bedecked in their totem trappings. "You slog out there to nothin'." He waved his arm.

"Worse than nothin'," Max said. He got slowly to his feet and walked with deliberate strides to stand beside Slake, his eyes as bleak as winter as he looked at Savan-

nah. "The first place you'll find is a sleaze-pit called
Bartertown. If the earth don't swallow you, sure as hell
that will." His voice grated with memory.

Savannah turned and shoved her way between them,
refusing to listen, refusing even to look at him. She strode
off through the Tribe toward the waiting steps.

"There ain't no Tomorrow-morrow-Land," Slake
shouted. "Lissen him!"

Savannah looked back, her hands clenched. "We done
that," she said, her eyes smoldering with betrayal as she
glanced at Max. "He's got wordstuff from his ass to his
mouth." She turned away again in disgust, heading up
the trail that led out of the canyon. Without looking back
she called, "Whoever's got the juice, track with us."
Cusha, Mr. Skyfish, and Finn McKoo followed; Gekko
began to hobble after them.

A dozen or so more Tribe members began to follow
her, tentatively, and then more, confidently. Slake stood
watching them go, as helpless as if he had suddenly
grown roots.

Max jerked the empty rifle from Slake's shoulder and
tore off the spear that was lashed to its barrel. Reaching
out to the gong, he yanked a handful of cartridges from
the chimes dangling beside it. He pushed two of the
bullets into the rifle's chamber with practiced fingers
while Slake stared at him uncomprehendingly.

Savannah and her followers were already halfway up
the steps. Max raised the loaded rifle and took aim. He
fired. The explosion of sound was followed by the crash as
a hanging urn shattered beside Savannah. Water poured
out of its ruined side, splashing on the rocks.

Everywhere around him the children screamed in terror and ran for their lives; little 'uns climbed up Slake

like squirrels up a tree. Even Scrooloose, watching from high above, darted back into his cave and hid.

Only Savannah stood her ground, her hands still clenched at her sides. Mr. Skyfish, Gekko, and several of her followers cowered among the rocks around her. Slake stood silently, still covered with trembling children, his face filled with sick awe as he realized at last what kind of man was standing in their midst with the eyes of a wild animal. Compared to this man, he knew no more than the little 'uns clinging to his arms, and never would.

"Now listen good!" Max shouted. "I ain't Captain Walker. I'm the guy who keeps Mr. Dead in his pocket." He held up the rifle. "And I say we're gonna stay here. We're gonna live a long time. And we're gonna be thankful! Right?"

Savannah turned her back on him again and kept walking. Slake watched her go, his sudden respect for her courage matched only by his disbelief at her foolhardiness.

Max took aim and fired again. The killing sound echoed earsplittingly from the rocks. This time the shot ruptured a melon in a basket beside Savannah's head; Savannah winced as wet rind splattered her shoulder.

Without hesitation and without warning Savannah spun around, her own arm up, her spear-thrower flashing faster than the eye could see. The spear hissed toward Max, buried itself in the dirt between his feet. Grimly Max pushed it aside, starting forward.

Two more spears thwacked into the ground on either side of him. Max stopped, looking down at his feet and up again. Cusha and Mr. Skyfish stood on the rocks above Savannah now, joining her heedless defiance. Savannah turned her back on Max for the final time, calling out to the others, "Keep trackin'!"

Gekko and Finn McKoo emerged from hiding, followed Cusha and Mr. Skyfish up the trail after Savannah.

Max threw down the rifle furiously and ran after them up the steps.

Savannah spun around, another spear raised and ready. Max tackled her, knocking the weapon from her hand, backhanding her across the face as she began to bite and struggle. "Slake!" he bellowed over his shoulder. "Grab 'em!"

Slake and the Hunters ran up the steps after him, bringing down Savannah's followers and dragging them back into camp again. Max hauled Savannah after them; even half stunned, she still punched and struggled.

Up above, Scrooloose emerged from his cave again at the sound of shouts and struggle. He stared down at the pandemonium below, as silent as a cloud, unnoticed and unremembered. Slowly he withdrew again into the darkness of his cave. He sat cross-legged among his gathered skulls, his eyes haunted and his face full of woe. With trembling hands he reached for his hide portrait of Walker. Pulling it down from the altar, he sank his teeth into its edge, ripped off a corner, and began to chew.

Obeying Max's commands with a haste born of mingled respect and fear, Slake and the Hunters tied Savannah's rebels up together and left them sitting in the sun like a disgruntled octopus. By tomorrow or the next day, Max figured, a taste of real hunger and thirst would have cooled their tempers to the point where Slake's reasoning or his own threats would be enough to make them admit that their plan was crazy.

Savannah was another matter. Max tied the cursing, kicking girl up himself, hand and foot, running the rope around a boulder for good measure. He gagged her with a strip of cloth to shut her up, as much to have a little peace and quiet as to keep her from swaying the others with her pleas. He recognized the look in her eyes, recognized an emotion he knew far too well burning inside her like cold fire.

And then he left her, and the rest of them, alone. The other children, even Slake and the Hunters, skittered out of his way everywhere he went, staring after him in wide-eyed silence, as if a mad dog had come to live in their camp. He went about his own business unconcernedly, eating, drinking, resting in the shade. Yesterday he'd been a god to them; today he was the devil. Tomorrow . . . tomorrow they'd begin to forget today, and when he left them alone, eventually he'd be no more remarkable here than a stone or a tree. They'd leave him alone, too, which was just what he wanted.

All except Savannah. He didn't know much about teenage rebellion, but he knew the kind of obsession that drove her now, the fury born when somebody killed your dreams. She was only a kid, and the dream was only a phantom . . . she hadn't lost everything. She was still surrounded by people who loved her and all the civilization anybody needed. One of these days she'd come to her senses and realize that. In the back of his mind he even admitted to a grudging admiration for her guts. She had the intelligence and the strength to be a real leader of the Tribe someday, if he could just keep her from committing suicide in the desert before she grew up.

Max built a small fire as dusk deepened and broiled two freshly caught fish; he shared nuts and berries with the monkey, who put in an appearance at his side for the first time all day. The monkey wandered away again into the shadows, clutching a handful of dates as he finished eating—headed back into the arms of some kid or other.

Max watched it go with a twinge of jealously. But he could hardly blame it for preferring the company of a score of worshiping children to his own. He didn't much like his own company, either, when he thought about it. He glanced at Savannah, still tied securely to the rock and scowling into the gathering darkness; looked away at the other rebels sitting uncomfortably in a bunch by the central fire pit. The girl Anna Goanna sat beside them, changing the dressing on her boyfriend's leg.

Max sighed, feeling the comfortable lethargy of a good meal and a hard but satisfying day begin to settle over him. Around him the older children were already shooing the younger ones off to bed. Still only half able to believe that for once he did not have to sleep with one eye open, he stretched out on the warm ground beside the fire and allowed himself the luxury of giving in to fatigue. He was asleep within minutes.

Unguarded sleep was something that he had banished from his life years ago and, with it, the treacherous ambush of memory. But on this night, asleep beneath the rustling trees in the heart of the quiet camp, he dreamed.

And woke, somewhere in the night, remembering the dream. He blinked, his eyes filling up with darkness and stars. He sat up, searching the black silence around him in sudden confusion as he found himself alone. "Jessie?" The single word escaped him, a raw whisper of agonized protest . . . the name he had not spoken in twenty years, because to speak it would have torn his throat apart like broken glass, and he would have bled to death inside.

But she had been *here,* lying beside him in the warm night—not the anguished ghost who drifted across his vision when he let his eyes wander, but the living, breathing woman, her face as fresh and vivid as if he had seen her only yesterday, not half a lifetime ago. He had held her in his arms again and kissed her . . . hugged the small, laughing boy with her face and his eyes, the living miracle they had created together . . . .

Max sagged forward, pressing his blistered face against his hands; raised his head again, touching his eyes in surprise. He wiped wetness from his fingers into the dirt.

He lay back again, staring up at the stars through the shifting branches of the trees. He hadn't seen his wife and child for twenty years—not living, breathing, smiling at him . . . not even in his dreams. He had lost them, they were—*Say it. Say it*—*dead.* Destroyed. Butchered. Nothing left of them but the image, burned into his brain with a white-hot iron, of their bodies lying like the crushed remains of some animal on the road he had pledged to defend; butchered by renegade bikers, by the same human animals who had killed his partner . . . the same ones he had thought he was saving the world from. In the end he hadn't even been able to save his own family.

The memories came now, and he couldn't stop them. He had gotten the bastards who had done it, given them exactly what they deserved, made certain that they would never hurt anyone else again. But it hadn't changed anything, hadn't even mattered by then . . . because nothing he could do could bring back his wife or his child, not even for a second. His own life had come to an end with theirs—prematurely—while civilization's sanity was still crumbling, just before it had committed its own murder.

When it had finally blown itself to hell a few weeks later, it had only seemed fitting. He had taken off alone into the wastes, and he had lived there ever since, never knowing why he bothered, never letting himself stop moving for long enough to question his own survival.

Punishing himself . . . a life sentence played out in a living death. Never letting himself get close enough to another human being to feel anything for them, because in this post-holocaust hell he was one of the walking damned, who would fail them, betray them . . . lose them. He had served his term in hell, becoming the kind of human animal he had always despised, no different from the ones who had destroyed the ones he loved. It was no wonder the Tribe acted like he was crazy.

Max sucked in a deep, uneven breath, and another one; forced himself to close his burning eyes. He relaxed his rigid body mechanically, as he had learned to do so long ago. The life he had once known—the woman, the child—had been as much of a lost dream for him as civilization was for the children of the Tribe. But his time in hell was over. For the first time in half a lifetime he had been able to dream about the past . . . and it had been a good dream. Maybe, given enough time, he could learn to let go of his own dream time and start over, like the children . . . learn to live again like a human being.

After a time his heartbeat slowed, and his breathing grew even and deep. He sighed, shifting onto his side, and let himself drift, feeling the peace of the whispering night settle over him again, feeling the darkness.

CHAPTER 13

THE SEARCH

Max woke with a start, with someone's hands on his shoulder, shaking him awake. Blinking sleep from his eyes, he looked up into the anguished face of Anna Goanna. "He's gone," she said sobbing. "You gotta get him back."

Him . . . her boyfriend—Gekko? Max raised his head, looking around the camp. It was full day already, but the village was deserted again. The hog-tied rebels were nowhere in sight. And Savannah was gone.

"Savannah took him—took 'em all," Anna said, tears running down her face.

Max took a deep breath. "Who let 'em loose?" he asked.

"Scrooloose," Anna said.

Max half frowned. "Who?"

Anna touched her head, circled her finger in the air.

Max had a sudden image of the kid with eyes like a raccoon, who hid in some cranny in the wall all day long. He grimaced. Scrambling to his feet, he began to run toward the steps, Anna Goanna running after him.

As Max reached the top of the canyon he heard an eerie wailing filling the air, found Slake and most of the Tribe still there, standing motionless on the sand, staring out past the wrecked 747, looking toward the Devil's Anvil. The desert beyond was empty for as far as he could see—except for a trail of footprints leading away toward the horizon. Slake turned back with pathetic eagerness as he approached.

"How long?" Max asked, shielding his eyes as he followed the tracks toward the horizon.

Slake shrugged unhappily. "Half a night—maybe less."

Max looked back at him. "They can't be far."

"They be doin' hunter trot," Slake said flatly.

"Not Gekko," Anna Goana protested. "His leg ain't healed."

"Good." Max nodded. "He'll slow 'em up." One of the girls had been pregnant too.

"It won't." Slake shook his head. "That's hunter law— stand or fall."

Stand or fall. The law of the wilderness. Maybe some of them would even make it across the desert to the other side, where there were no laws at all. Unless somebody went after them. Max stared at five sets of footprints and the tracks of a sledge leading away into hell.

Anna Goanna's face crumpled. "You gotta bring him back. You gotta, Captain!"

Max turned on her, frowning. "Don't call me Captain." Behind him, stretching away along the dune, the Tribe kept up its wailing. None of them had gone after the runaways into the Nothing...and none of them would. He glanced at Slake, saw the fear and the guilt on the boy's face. He'd done too good a job on them.

Max turned back, looking out into the glaring furnace of light. The sun beat down on his unprotected head; its heat was dizzying. Hell lay waiting patiently ... holding hostages. Max's hands tightened into fists. He looked at Slake again. "I'll need water—as much as I can carry."

Anna Goanna's face filled with sudden relief. Slake nodded and raised his hand. The wailing stopped as Tribe members began to come forward one by one, dropping their water bags into a pile. Max stood silently, listening to the skin bags plop to the ground behind him. As the last of the bottles was deposited at his feet, he turned back again. Kneeling down, he picked them up one by one and slung them over his shoulder. As he loaded himself up a pair of slim legs crossed his line of vision. Anna Goanna bent down beside him and began to pick up water bags.

Max looked up, frowning again. "What are you doing?"

She stuck her chin out, frowning back at him. "I's coming salvage for my buddy!"

Max hesitated a moment and then nodded. He stood up, pulling more water bags up over his shoulder.

Anna turned to Slake. "We needs a Hunter!"

Slake looked expectantly at the Hunters gathered around him. One by one they hung their heads or glanced away, their faces pinched with shame and fear.

Anna's face twisted with disgust. She turned back to the pile of remaining bags to pick up more. As she leaned down a pair of small, chubby hands were there before her. Eddie began to pick up water bottles, following her example with a happy smile.

"No!" A larger hand entered her line of sight, shooing Eddie back. She looked up to find Tubba Tintye, the fat kid who was always last in line when Slake and the Hunters took the trail. She had always thought he was a chickenshit. She raised her eyebrows in surprise. Tubba shrugged resignedly, half smiling, and picked up another water bag.

Max started away across the sand without a word, knowing that Anna and Tubba were following him only by the scuff of their footsteps. Above, the Tribe watched them go, equally silent now. Eddie peered forlornly between the legs of the shamefaced Hunters.

Max and the two kids trekked on into the desert, Crack in the Earth melting into the heat haze behind them like a mirage. Max kept his eyes on the tracks ahead, never letting himself look back, trying not to think at all. As they slogged up the face of another dune he heard a cry, very faint, seeming to come from all four quarters of the distance. Max scrambled to the top of the next ridge, looking ahead, searching for the cry's source, hoping against hope. . . . Behind him, Tubba tried to speak; Max waved him to silence, listening.

Another cry came. Max searched the horizon, seeing nothing anywhere. Tubba tapped him insistently on the shoulder. Max looked back impatiently. Cresting the dune behind them was tiny Eddie, struggling valiantly to catch up, his battered teddy bear clutched in his arms and a single container of water flopping at his back.

Max swore furiously and plunged on down the face of the dune. "He holds his own, okay?"

Eddie held his own, much to Max's surprise, with a little help from Tubba and Anna. The fact did not improve his mood. Anna Goanna wanted Gekko back— they all wanted Savannah and her band of rebels back, or what the hell were they doing out here?—but the kids treated this search like some kind of goddamn Boy Scout hike. They didn't know what they were getting into, any more than Savannah did. Max trudged on, his clenched jaw aching with tension, wishing that he didn't know, either.

They followed Savannah's trail all through the day, never seeing anything ahead but footprints leading them deeper into the desert. Max pressed on at the best speed he could hold; his own strength was still limited, but if they didn't find the others soon, they might just as well never have begun this journey . . . and none of them would ever see Crack in the Earth again. Anna Goanna and Tubba had no trouble matching his pace, even with Eddie in tow; their bare legs and moccasined feet seemed to be impervious to the sand's blistering heat. They drank little and let him feel their impatience with his own progress. Max said nothing, saving his strength, sinking back into the silent emptiness of the void.

As the sun sank low in the west, the wind began to rise, lifting languid curls of dust. Grimly Max pushed on, pushing himself harder, knowing all too well what the rising wind would do to the tracks they followed. If they lost Savannah's trail, they'd never pick it up again. They kept on through the night, tracking by moonlight, not stopping for sleep, and by dawn Tubba told him that they were gaining.

They pushed deeper into the salt-crusted wastes of the Devil's Anvil, beneath the pitiless gaze of another day's rising sun. The heat rang like a hammer on the glittering surface of the lake bed. The specter of his own agonizing journey across this land of death swam like a mirage across his vision. Resolutely he kept his eyes on the way ahead, the tracks already fading as the wind strength-

ened. Savannah Nix had saved his life from the thing
that waited here; he wasn't going to let it claim hers
instead.

But their own pace slowed more and more; he was the
one who dragged or carried Eddie up the dunes now.
Anna Goanna and Tubba had grown grim and silent,
lagging behind him, their lips cracked, their footsteps
dragging, their skin burned crimson. Max had slogged it
on will alone before; they were tough kids, but their life
had been soft until now, and realizing it only made their
going harder. His only hope lay in the signs that Savannah's band was slowing even more—Gekko's leg had to
be the reason, but Savannah hadn't abandoned him . . .
not yet. Max squinted ahead, sand and dust stinging his
face, past and present shifting places and shifting back
again as he bent forward against the wind, following a
trail that might lie only in his imagination.

Beside him Anna Goanna gave a cry, ran forward as
she spotted something lying in the sand ahead. Max
began to run, too, as he saw what she held up—Gekko's
forked stick, the phonograph record still wedged onto one
branch. Anna scrambled on again, climbing the next rise,
shouting, "Gekko! Gekko!" She disappeared over the top.

Max reached the top of the dune behind her and
stopped, looking down. Below them a solitary figure
crawled in hopeless circles in the sand, groping futilely,
searching for something. Gekko. Anna plunged and slid
down the face of the dune to his side, calling his name.

He turned, looking up at her cry, his blistered face
anguished, his gaze wandering aimlessly, dazzled by the
glare of sun on sand. Anna reached his side and dropped
down beside him, grabbing his shoulders. He twisted,
struggling in her hold, not even seeming to recognize her;

his eyes were glassy with fever. "The sonic!" he whimpered, "I's lost the sonic!"

Anna pushed the forked stick into his hands, tears filling her own eyes. She pulled a water bag off her shoulder and unstoppered it, holding it to his lips.

Max stood with Tubba and Eddie on the ridge, watching through the wavering fog of heat and dust as the two figures merged into one in the valley below. He stared at them for a long moment with shadowed eyes before he started down the hill.

With the help of Tubba, Max lashed together a litter of spears and hides like the one that had carried him to Crack in the Earth. Together they loaded the helpless boy onto it, still clutching his stick to his chest, and tied him in place. Max leaned down, not meeting Anna's eyes as he slung the litter's straps over his shoulders.

The sandstorm grew worse as they went on. The sun seemed to hang motionless behind its veil of dust and sand as the afternoon became an eternity of struggling forward and sliding back, climbing and falling, moving through the long-dead sea like swimmers under water. Dazed with exhaustion, slowed by the burden of Gekko, Max and the trackers continued to lose ground.

At last, cresting another wave in the endless sea of dunes, Max stopped short, staring out at the desert ahead. And saw nothing at all. The trail of footprints had vanished, swept away completely by the storm. The small band stood uncertainly, each one looking in a different direction, searching for some trace, some sign. No one spoke, afraid to give that much power to their fears.

Suddenly Eddie pulled at Max's arm, pointing up into the sky with a gleeful grin. Very high up, something was flying, wheeling and circling on the currents of heated air.

"Yeah," Max murmured, his voice thick with dust.
"It's a hawk."

Tubba looked up, squinting at the strange motion of
the bird. "That ain't bird-rafting," he said with sudden
excitement. "That's Mr. Skyfish!" Around Max all the
children broke into smiles for the first time. They started
on at a jog-trot, the sight of it giving them fresh strength.

Reaching the last rise, they slithered to a stop again,
their gaze following the kite string down. Max's heart
sank into his boots.

Below them lay Mr. Skyfish, the kite tethered to his
wrist . . . lying spread-eagle on the sand, clinging to
Cusha's arm: the anchor for a human chain that
stretched to the bottom of the dune where Savannah lay,
desperately clutching a strip of hide.

Holding on to the other end was Finn McKoo, up to his
neck in the same kind of sinkhole that had swallowed the
dead horse.

Max unslung the straps of the litter and sprinted
across the sand, running toward the sinkhole. As he ran
he watched Finn sink up to his chin, past it, screaming in
terror as he fought to keep his mouth clear. The leather
strap strained, stretching. . . . Finn disappeared, dragging
the leather and Savannah after him into the sand.

Scrooloose fought frantically to keep his hold on
Savannah's ankle, his own hands slipping as she was
dragged forward, straining the entire human chain to its
breaking point. Abruptly it snapped as Scrooloose's other
hand lost its grip on Cusha's ankle. Scrooloose and
Savannah slithered down into the funnel of sand, Savannah still clinging fiercely to the strip of hide as she was
dragged headfirst into the hole.

Max dove down the slope and caught Scrooloose's
flailing hand. Scrambling for a purchase, he pulled

Scrooloose back and up with all his strength. Behind him he felt someone's hands lock over his ankles, joining their weight to his own. Savannah's shoulders began to reappear, and then her head, inch by inch, as they dragged her free from the embrace of the desert, barely conscious but still alive. The leather strap slid out of the sand, Savannah's fingers still knotted convulsively around it. Its other end emerged from the sinkhole, flapping loose. Finn McKoo was gone.

Cautiously the human chain inched back up the slope until they all sat together, safe on its rim, whimpering with exhaustion and horror. Savannah lay motionless, staring with haunted eyes at something unspeakable, her empty hands clenching and unclenching.

Beside them on the rim of the slope was the rough sled she had used to haul their water and supplies across the desert. Tubba roused himself at last as he noticed it beside him. Collecting the water bags his own band had been carrying on their backs for so long, he plunked them down on the sled. He settled back again, relieved to be rid of the burden.

And behind him, the overbalanced sled began to tip and to slide. . . .

Mr. Skyfish sat up with a cry; Tubba spun around, too late to stop it as it pitched over the rim and down. Max scrambled to his feet, leaping forward, too late. He watched as the desert claimed its fee for trespass a second time, as the sled spiraled down the slope like a falling leaf and disappeared silently into the bottomless maw of the sand pit with every drop of water they possessed.

Max and the band stood together for a long time, staring down the slope at nothing at all, while the full measure of their loss ate its way through their minds like acid. Max glanced at Savannah, who stood apart from the others, her eyes bleak but without tears. Finn McKoo had been her own child. In the communal family of the Tribe all the older ones treated all the little 'uns as their own; but she would have died with him before she would have let him go.

Silently Savannah reached down, taking in her hands the small, battered globe of the world she wore slung at her waist. She unscrewed it and carefully removed what lay inside—an emu egg filled with water. She gave it to Eddie, who took a sip and passed it to Mr. Skyfish.

Mr. Skyfish shook his head, glancing away toward where Anna Goanna crouched beside the litter, cradling Gekko's head in her arms, shielding him from the wind-driven sand. "Give it to Gekko." He passed the egg to Cusha, who shook her own head and passed it to Scrooloose, who gave it to Anna Goanna. She pressed it to Gekko's lips.

He opened his eyes and turned his face away. "No . . . no," he whispered. "We's gonna need it later."

"C'mon, Gekko," Savannah urged softly, crouching down beside him. "We's got plenty. Drink."

Gekko took the egg in trembling hands and drained it, settling back with a sigh.

The wind gusted suddenly, wailing like a chorus of lost souls, making them stagger. Sand blew into their eyes, into their noses and mouths, scouring their exposed skin. One by one the children crouched down again, defeated, turning their backs to the storm. Max settled down among them as they huddled together, sharing what little protection they could, while time and the desert closed in around them.

The sun grew weary in time, rolling down the sky toward its night of rest. Even the wind grew weary at last and laid down its burden of sand, breathing gently. Sand poured from hunched, motionless backs and shoulders as Gekko crawled forward, heading out across the quiet desert toward the top of a nearby rise.

"I can hear it," he called. His sunken, fever-bright eyes were fixed on the sunset horizon. "I's hearing the sonic."

Anna Goanna roused from her half stupor, half sleep at the sound of his voice. She shook herself off and stumbled to her feet, starting after him.

"It's there," Gekko cried as she caught up with him, lending him the strength of her supporting arm. "I's hearing it."

Anna looked out with him across the dunes, searching in vain for whatever he saw, listening for what he heard. Her breath caught, her own eyes suddenly widening in disbelief. A long way off, almost to the horizon, pillars of smoke were rising into the sky. As she watched, blinking and blinking again, the fading sunset glow suddenly flared up again, shimmering like the aurora borealis, illuminating the pillars of smoke until they shone like a spirit vision. "Home . . ." Gekko murmured, "home." Anna sucked in her breath in amazement. "Captain! Captain!" she cried. "We's there."

Max shook himself free of the sand and climbed to his feet. Around him the other children began to stir and sit up. Squinting at the uncanny glow like a fallen star beyond the dunes, he limped forward to the place where Anna Goanna and Gekko stood silhouetted side by side. As he reached the top of the rise his stomach twisted with sudden recognition. The children trailed after him one by one, until they all stood beside him, their eyes wide with wonder; all of them smiling . . . except Savannah—and Max.

"Bartertown," Max said at last, spitting out the word. Behind him Mr. Skyfish picked up a spear and drove it hard into the ground. With deft fingers he tied the string of his kite to it. The kite began to drift upward on the back of the breeze, the silk and feather bird-form rising into the sky like a spirit. "That be Finn's marker," Mr. Skyfish said softly, "And the bird be his eyes, watching over us all." He turned away, looking behind them. "So long, Finn McKoo." Savannah bit her lip, turning her face toward the glowing beacon on the horizon.

Together the small band started on across the desert, heading for Bartertown.

CHAPTER 14

THIRTY-THREE POLES

They reached the thirty-three poles sometime before dawn. Max stood silently on the salt flats below Bartertown, staring up at his own funeral marker freshly erected beside the other thirty-two. The skull at its tip returned his stare with a hollow-eyed grin, welcoming him home.

Max turned away again with a sigh of resignation, looking back at Anna Goanna somberly tending Gekko at the foot of a nearby pole. Gekko was in bad shape. The boy needed more than they could give him ... maybe more than anybody could give him now. Max glanced at Savannah, sitting cross-legged nearby, silent and unmoving—out of all the rest, the only one who seemed indifferent to their arrival. Her eyes flickered up, meeting Max's gaze as she felt him look at her. There was no hatred in her stare now, no betrayal ... only desolation, the emptiness of the wasteland. She believed him now . . . and he was only sorry.

Max looked away from her. There were some things only experience could teach, and most of them were things you didn't want to know. He nodded to the rest of the Tribe, who stood waiting impatiently for their first glimpse of what lay beyond the top of the ridge. He had known that he couldn't keep them from looking, at least, but he had forbidden any of them to get out of his sight. The only way they'd ever understand about Bartertown was by learning the hard way, and he was damned if a single one of them was going to end up any wiser tonight. One look was all they were getting, and then they were going home.

Max started up the slope, the kids following, treading softly. He had to reconnoiter if he was going to find a way back in, and he had to find a way back in if he was going to steal enough water for their return to Crack in the Earth. The only thing he'd get if he showed his face at Entity's gates fresh from Gulag was an arrow in his gut; but the monkey had gotten out somehow, and so somewhere there had to be another way to get inside. He cursed himself for not bringing the rifle. He had never believed that any of them would get this far. Just his luck.

The glow of Bartertown's lights blotted out the stars as Max reached the top of the hill and flattened himself on its rim. The kids imitated his every move, lying down beside him. They were on the cliffs above the town. From here they could look straight down into the central square. Entity's penthouse was directly opposite their eye level; Max could see shadowed figures moving behind the flowing gauze-curtained walls. All around the tower Bartertown was hopping; the shouts and laughter and wrangling carried clearly in the still desert air. Thunderdome's sign was flashing, and a fair crowd was gathering outside it. He wondered who would be getting killed in there tonight.

The kids gazed down on Bartertown, their breath hissing in a group gasp of wonder. And then the words came pouring out of half a dozen mouths at once.

"We's there!"

"Tomorrow-morrow-Land."

"Where's the video?"

"They got their own stars."

"We's home."

"Morrow-Land!"

"A high-scraper!"

Max gestured fiercely, trying to silence them. "Shut up," he rasped. "It's not Tomorrow-Land. It's Bartertown." He looked out and down again as a movement partway down the cliff caught his eye: a unit of Entity's Imperial Guards on patrol. He tugged sharply on shoulders and ankles, forcing the Tribe to back off, herding them back down the ridge into the darkness.

It was like trying to herd mice; no sooner had he gotten the last one pried loose and sliding down the hill than Mr. Skyfish was back at the top. Max caught hold of the boy's arm again and shoved him ungently after the others. Risking a final glance over his shoulder, Max saw the silhouette of a woman's figure, very clearly outlined behind the gauze of Entity's penthouse.

He slid hastily down the hill after the kids, halting them halfway down the slope and doing a rapid head count.

One short. "Where's What's-his-name?" he snapped. They looked at him blankly.

"You know——?" he said impatiently, making the crazy sign beside his head.

They looked at each other now, realizing suddenly that Scrooloose was gone.

"Not just him," Mr. Skyfish said. "Co-pilot's gone the lost. . ."

Co-pilot? After a moment he remembered that they meant his monkey. He hadn't seen any trace of it since he'd met up with Savannah's group. Anger and exasperation struggled for first place in his mind. Goddamn stupid kids—on top of everything else, they'd taken his goddamned monkey, too, and now they'd lost it again. He swore with useless frustration, shepherding them down to the bottom of the hill.

Max looked around in the darkness, searching for Scrooloose as they gathered again beneath the thirty-three poles . . . nearly jumped out of his skin as a hand fell on his shoulder from behind. He spun around to find Scrooloose's wild, grinning face staring up into his own like a jack-o'-lantern.

Scrooloose took hold of his arm, tugged on it with obvious urgency, trying to force Max to follow.

"All right, all right," Max said, taking a step forward. He stopped, looked back at the others. "You lot—stay here." He put up his hand, palm out, glaring a threat at them as he followed Scrooloose away into the darkness.

A dozen yards along the foot of the hill Scrooloose stopped again and pointed ahead proudly. In a shallow cul-de-sac the dark mouth of a drain pipe *oh'd* in surprise, drooling a thin stream of seepage. The monkey sat perched on top of it, chittering happily as it spotted them. So this was the secret entrance. . . . The monkey must have gone on ahead when the others got into trouble, knowing what they could not—that Bartertown was just over the horizon. "Good," Max muttered, nodding. Scrooloose grinned even wider, obviously pleased with himself. Max wasn't sure how much the crazy kid understood, but maybe it was more than he'd given him credit for. "Now wait," he said quietly but firmly. "Wait here— understand? I'll get the others."

He turned away; jerked to a halt as he found himself face-to-face with every single one of the others except Savannah, Anna Goanna, and Gekko . . . all of them standing and watching his reaction with wide-eyed interest.

Max took a deep breath and said with murderous intensity, "Everybody waits here! Get it?" Leaning down, he picked up a stick and held it out to Scrooloose. "Use this. The first person who moves—belt 'em." He pressed the stick into Scrooloose's waiting hand. "Understand?"

Scrooloose nodded earnestly.

Max turned away.

The length of wood came down on his head with a resounding whack. The other children jumped back in surprise.

Max shook his head, more in disbelief than in pain, looking over his shoulder. Scrooloose stood before the drainpipe, thumping the stick on his open palm like a nightwatchman. Max sighed heavily and started back along the base of the hill.

Anna Goanna and Savannah were both crouched beside Gekko now, trying to tend him, with nothing to ease his suffering but the comfort of their hands. Max stood over them, looking down at the boy. Gekko's eyes were glazed, his blistered face wet with sweat, his breathing shallow; he was muttering to himself, incoherent words and phrases.

Anna Goanna looked up, tears running down her face again. "He's talkin' to Mr. Dead."

Max's hands tightened helplessly, opened again. He kneeled down beside them.

Gekko's wandering eyes fixed on his face. "That you, Captain?" he mumbled. "We's there?"

Max gathered the boy up gently in his arms; the thin, fever-wasted body scarcely seemed to weigh anything as he lifted it. Carrying him easily, Max began to climb the hill again toward the lights of Bartertown. This time Anna and Savannah followed him.

Max reached the crest of the hill and dropped to his knees with infinite care, lowering Gekko, supporting the boy's head against his shoulder as he pointed at the lights below. Savannah and Anna Goanna crouched down beside them, looking out at the lights and back again in wonder as Gekko tried to focus his eyes. An expression of uncertain awe filled his face.

"I sees it," he whispered. "I sees the river of light." He struggled to lift his head, gazing across at Entity's penthouse, a glowing, amorphous shape floating in the air. He reached out for it, stretching his arms. "Skyraft—they's skyrafting." He looked up at Max. "We's there, ain't we?" he murmured eagerly. "Tomorrow-morrow-Land."

Max nodded. "Yes, son," he said softy. Gekko shifted in his arms, looking toward Anna Goanna.

"But where's the sonic?" he said. "I can't get no sonic."

Quickly Anna put his forked stick into his hands and slipped the headphones onto his ears. He listened for a long moment, straining. "It ain't there." He pulled the headphones off. "I ain't gonna hear it. . ." He pushed the headphones back into Anna Goanna's hands. "But you will. You'll hear it for me." Fumbling, his hand spun the old LP . . . dropped suddenly onto her hand, and lay still.

Max held the boy close for a moment longer before he was certain that the hand would never move again, that Gekko was really free at last to go after his dream. Gekko's eyes still stared out at the lights of Bartertown; Max made no move to close them.

Max swallowed with difficulty, forced himself to look up at Anna Goanna's face. "You want me to bury him?" he asked at last.

She shook her head.

Max, Savannah, and Anna Goanna made their way slowly back down the ridge, Anna carrying the old LP. She looked up one last time at Gekko's body, silhouetted by the lights of Bartertown: He sat cross-legged, his forked stick in his hand, still staring out at the river of light.

Max led Savannah and Anna silently back through the alley of skulls, along the hill to the drain opening; stopped short as he reached it. Nobody stood there waiting for him; the rest of the Tribe had disappeared.

"Shit." Max lifted his hands in a spasm of exasperation; looked from side to side, searching the darkness around him for what seemed like the thousandth time.

Abruptly Tubba's head popped out of the drain. The round-faced kid glanced over his shoulder, pointed back into the drain with his thumb, and disappeared.

Max shepherded Savannah and Anna Goanna into the drain with heavy reluctance and started after them. As he stepped into the drainpipe he hesitated, realizing that he could actually see what he was doing. He glanced back over his shoulder.

Thirty-three poles rose like mourners in black silhouette before him. The first light of a new day had broken in the east. Somewhere to the east was Crack in the Earth. For a brief span of heartbeats Max watched the sun rise, its fluid face enormous and blood-red, before he turned back, following the others into the darkness.

CHAPTER 15

THE FALL OF BARTERTOWN

Max followed Savannah and Anna Goanna through the tunnel, the ruddy dawn lighting their way. Savannah crawled past a large side pipe; Anna hesitated, turning into it as if she had decided to explore. Max grabbed her roughly, pushing her back down the main drain. Ahead of them the drainpipe curved; Savannah disappeared from his sight. As he followed the others around the bend he suddenly saw the drain's end ahead—blocked by a grid of iron bars. Cusha and Tubba sat there, both of them too big around to squeeze through the grate. Cusha held the monkey in her arms; she smiled happily when she saw Savannah.

Max and Anna joined them, crouching in front of the bars. "Where are the others?" Max said, already guessing where they'd gone. *For Christ's sake, why couldn't something be simple just once?*

Cusha pointed forlornly through the bars, into Underworld. Max pushed closer to the grate, looking out.

Beyond and below him was the familiar reeking sea of pigs. He saw no human figures moving among them yet; probably it was still too early for even convicts or slaves to be up and working. In the middle of the hogs, in a small pen of his own, lay Elvis Ford—once the Master of Underworld, now living like an animal, guarded by animals . . . four-legged and two-legged. Max's gaze moved on to the platform surrounding the locomotive engine. Ironbar Bassey stood there, already awake or still awake from the night before, his totem face bobbing above the heads of three other Imperial Guards, two men and a woman.

Ironbar and the tallest, heaviest Guard were standing face-to-face, each with one arm planted on a table, playing at the most bizarre version of an arm-wrestling game Max had ever seen. Each man had hold of a handle attached to a system of chains and pulleys; whoever pulled down the hardest would yank his opponent's hand up into the bed of spikes waiting above. Max grimaced, looking up at the spikes. Of all the asshole ways to pass time . . . His eyes wandered; his face froze.

High up in the maze of pipes and cables above the platform a spectator sat, watching avidly: Scrooloose. Scrooloose glanced up, saw Max glaring at him, waved and looked down again.

Max looked back at the Guards, speechless. Ironbar was psyching out his opponent, staring him straight in the eye, humming a cheerful off-key ditty. The other Guard tried to meet Ironbar's gaze, sweating now, his own face twitching with strain and tension.

Ironbar smiled, sublimely confident, and pulled a little harder.

The muscleman's nerve snapped. With a sudden vicious yank Ironbar sent the Guard's hand flying up into the waiting spikes. The Guard howled; his companions cheered loudly and unsympathetically.

So did Scrooloose.

Ironbar and the Guards looked up into the plumbing, frowning with surprise and confusion. Scrooloose pulled deeper into the shadows as Max signaled him back frantically.

Max looked down at the Guards again, holding his breath. They stood shrugging, exchanging puzzled stares; slowly they went back to their game, chalking it up to a peculiar echo.

This time the woman Guard stepped forward and took hold of one of the handles. She was nearly a head taller than Ironbar and had more muscles than Max had ever seen on a woman. Ironbar smiled, unimpressed, and took hold of the other bar with his teeth. At a signal from the remaining undamaged Guard, they began a new round of tug-of-war.

Max slumped back from the grating with a sigh. Scrooloose was in his sight and safe, for the moment at least. That left Mr. Skyfish and Eddie unaccounted for. "Okay, now where are the other two?"

Everyone shrugged.

Max peered wearily through the grate again.

Beyond his sight on the other side of the cavern, Pig Killer sat on the edge of a hog pen, holding a squirming piglet under his arm, feeding the tiny orphan with a makeshift teat fastened onto an old beer bottle. He made a point of getting up early for this, the one thing in his day he had any reason to look forward to.

"Walker . . . Walker . . . ."

He glanced up as the incongruous sound of a child's high-pitched voice reached him over the noise of the pigs. He turned, looking down from his seat on the fence, to find a litle boy of four or five standing in the walkway, a teddy bear tied onto his back like a papoose, watching somberly. "Captain Walker?" the little boy said, with the sudden smile of an angel.

Pig Killer sat back, gaping with disbelief. "Where did you spring from?" he said at last, completely inadequately.

The little boy's smile widened. "Planet Erf?"

Pig Killer dropped the piglet back into the pen and slid down from the fence, looking nervously toward Ironbar's command platform as the little boy took his hand and began to lead him away through the pigs.

Up on the platform, totally oblivious, Ironbar was still engaged in his wrestling match with the woman Guard, which was not ending as abruptly as he had anticipated. The other two Guards watched, urging the wrestlers on, their eyes riveted on the straining bodies in front of them.

Max glanced back at them again, having searched the rest of his range of vision, finding nothing but pigs. The muscles and veins stood out on Ironbar's neck and shaven head now, bulging at his teeth pulled down on the handle like a bulldog's. Up above, Scrooloose leaned out over the edge of the boiler, his bared teeth clenched tight, mimicking the struggle.

Ironbar grunted loudly; Scrooloose grunted too, even louder. Ironbar looked up, losing his concentration. The woman Guard jerked down on her handle. Ironbar's head flew up, crashing into the spikes. He screamed, staggering back, clutching his torn, bleeding scalp.

But the other Guards were looking up now, peering

into the darkness among the overhead pipes again. Max saw their expessions freeze as they spotted Scrooloose. They ran for the access ladder, the woman leading the way.

Master stirred in his pen, awakened by Ironbar's scream. He climbed to his feet, peering over the fence and through the pigs toward the command platform where the Guards were climbing the ladder in pursuit of something.

Scrooloose looked down and saw the Guards climbing up. Max gestured frantically at him to run, climb, hide. But however Scrooloose had gotten up there, there was no easy way back. Scrooloose stood where he was, trapped and panic-stricken, looking down at the murderous hulks climbing after him in wild-eyed terror.

Max's fists tightened over the bars of the drainage grate and jerked impotently. Suddenly Ironbar turned, looking away from Scrooloose at something higher up in air. Max followed his gaze, watched in amazement as Mr. Skyfish sailed down out of the rafters like Tarzan, swinging from a chain.

Mr. Skyfish booted the woman Guard off the ladder and into the pigs, and landed deftly beside Scrooloose on top of the boiler. Scrooloose flung his arms around Mr. Skyfish's neck, and they swung away again together, heading straight for Max and the drainage tunnel.

Down below, Master stood on tiptoe in his pen, watching in equal incredulity as the two children soared by overhead. Turning to follow their progress, he unexpectedly came face-to-face with a being at his own eye level.

Eddie beamed with delight. "Captain Walker?" he cried eagerly.

Pig Killer raised a finger to his lips, shushing them both, pointing with his free hand.

Ironbar Bassey was climbing down from the platform, carrying a musket, followed by his two remaining Guards. One of them stopped to collect something—a huge pair of boltcutters—as they pushed through the pigs toward the drainpipe. Only the feet of Mr. Skyfish and Scrooloose were visible now as they wormed their way back inside.

The first Guard began to climb the access ladder leading up to the pipe, while Ironbar stood below, waiting impatiently for the cutters. The other Guard lagged far behind, dragging the heavy cutters as he struggled to catch up.

He stopped suddenly, looking back in sudden surprise, as someone tapped him on the shoulder. A shovel struck him square in the face as he turned, dropping him to the ground among the pigs. Pig Killer leaned down to pick up the shears, grinning with satisfaction.

Ironbar looked back again, just as Pig Killer leaned over. The Guard and the cutters had vanished. He frowned, looked up again, watching as the first Guard pulled himself up over the edge of the pipe and peered in through the grate.

A fist shot out of the drainpipe, smashing the Guard in the face. The Guard lost his grip, fell back and down, into the pigs. Furiously Ironbar raised his gun and fired into the mouth of the drainpipe.

The bullet splanged and ricocheted from the walls of the pipe as Max pushed the children back into the drain, flattening on top of them until the echoes stopped. He herded them up and on again, sending them down the side tunnel that Anna Goanna had tried to explore before. Looking back, he saw the sightless, leering face of Ironbar's totem peer in at him through the grille; he flung himself after the others, out of Bassey's line of sight.

Ironbar's own head filled the opening as Max disappeared; Ironbar glimpsed someone's retreating foot as he ducked out of sight. Scowling with frustration, Bassey dropped back to the ground, pushing through the hogs, tracking the pipe away across the cavern. Overhead he could hear the crunching passage of bodies crawling through the pig feed stored inside as Max and the children fumbled blindly in the darkness up above. Soon they'd reach the other end . . . and he'd be there, waiting.

Ironbar glanced away suddenly as an unexpected movement caught the corner of his eye. He turned to see a convict lifting Master out of his sleeping pen and onto the platform. Another kid stood up there already, waiting.

Pig Killer looked around tensely as he lifted Master onto the platform, following the little man's terse instructions. His eyes met Ironbar's glowering stare; he froze as Bassey's musket swung up, aiming right at his chest. Pig Killer flung up a gauntleted hand. "Hold it!" he shouted, yelling the first thing that came into his head. "Just remember—no matter where you go, there you are . . . ."

Ironbar hesitated, lowering his gun, his face blank with confusion. Up on the platform behind Pig Killer, Master leapt forward to the control panel and jerked down a lever.

As Ironbar raised his musket again a large overhead chute swung down from the pipe above his head with a squealing groan. He looked up, just as it fell. The end of it crashed down on his head, knocking him cold. Ironbar dropped to the ground, a torrent of pig food sluicing down on top of him, burying him.

Inside the pipe, Max and the Tribe scrambled futilely as the dried beans and fodder gave way beneath them

and sent them hurtling down in a dusty avalanche to the
floor below.

Max landed with a grunt on top of a pile of body-filled
pig feed, already surrounded by snuffling, grunting hogs.
He shook his vision clear, turned to see Pig Killer coming
toward the pile as fast as he could wade through pigs,
carrying the bolt cutters in his fist like a club.

Pig Killer stopped short as Max looked up at him; he
stared, his mouth hanging, the way a man would stare
who had just run into a ghost. Back on the platform
Master watched goggle-eyed as more and more children's
head began to pop up out of the pile of fodder, with the
man who had refused to take Blaster's life sitting dazed
in their midst. The children began to scramble up and
shake themselves off. Beside him Eddie waved happily to
his friends and moved to Master's side, putting his arm
around his new buddy, the first grown-up he had ever
seen who was just the right size.

Max picked himself up from the floor, Pig Killer and
the kids already beginning to fill the air around him with
clamoring questions.

"Quiet!" Max ordered, shutting them up with an
abrupt gesture. Somewhere in the distance he heard,
incongruously, the sound of someone singing "The
Toreador Song" from *Carmen*.

Blackfinger, Entity's chief mechanic, came striding
into the cavern on his way to work, his head covered by a
bandanna, his toolbox under his arm and his lunch box in
his hand, singing at the top of his voice as he headed
toward the garage. He glanced at Max and the odd crew
gathered around him, all staring back with tense, frozen
faces. He waved with absentminded good humor, too
nearsighted to notice anything strange about them. "Hi,

guys!" he called, breaking into song again as he strode on by.

Abruptly he slowed, stopped dead, looking down at something lying among the pigs. The body of a Guard. Still singing, he marked time for a step or two, then began to march backward, turned suddenly, and bolted out of the cavern.

Max ran after him, knowing that if they didn't stop him before he reached a place where he could give an alarm, they were finished.

Up on the platform Master rattled the chains that hung suspended from a runner on the ceiling, its other end welded to the steel collar around his neck. "Quickly!" he cried, gesturing Pig Killer and the bolt cutters up onto the platform. Pig Killer cut through the chain with a hard twist of the shears, setting Master free. Master beckoned the Tribe forward, taking command with a confidence born of long experience. "All of you—no questions. Just do as you're told." He began to point, giving orders, and the others scrambled to obey. He had spent hours—days—waking and sleeping, trying to imagine his escape from Underworld. Now that he had allies again, the time had come —and he knew precisely how to make it happen and take his revenge on Entity in the process.

Max raced after Blackfinger up a tunnel passageway. Blackfinger ran like the devil was on his tail, but slowly Max gained ground, almost on top of him as he darted through the narrow opening between the heavy wooden doors that sealed the way to Underworld. Max followed him, running uphill now through a culvert lined with bricks. Blackfinger disappeared around a bend in the tunnel. Max pounded after him, skidded to a halt as he found himself face-to-face with the grinning mechanic, flanked now by the Collector and two Guards.

Max turned on his heel and ran back the way he had come as if the devil were on his tail. He dodged back through the narrow opening between the doors, pulling up short again to push them shut.

But Savannah was already there, sliding one side shut for him even as he turned. Breathing hard, Max threw his weight against the other door, slamming it to. They pressed their backs to the wood, holding the gate shut as they searched for something to bar it.

With a tearing roar the blade of a chainsaw burst through the wood beside Max's head, sending chips flying as it began to rip its way inexorably down the door. Max stumbled back, barely saving his shoulder from the blade as he watched the hungry saw chew its way toward the floor.

A heavy metal bar shot across the wood toward him, dropped into its tracks just as the blade came down across its path. With a hideous scream the chainsaw bit into the metal and seized up, its chain snapping as the blade ground to a halt. Grimacing with satisfaction, Savannah gave the bar another shove, jamming it firmly into place, holding the door shut for good.

Max took a deep breath, nodded once in respect and thanks. A fleeting smile twitched Savannah's face. Together they started back down the tunnel. Max shook his head, muttering a curse. "What now?"

A sledgehammer crashed against the door behind them, making the wood jump. Max and Savannah began to move faster.

As they reentered the cavern the shrill echo of a train whistle sounded once, twice. Looking toward the sound, they saw everyone else on board the old locomotive. Pig

Killer sat in the cab with Cusha and Tubba beside him, holding onto the monkey. Eddie, Anna, Mr. Skyfish, and Scrooloose were clustered around Master's house on the flatbed car behind it; Master still stood on the platform up above. Everyone had their fingers stuck in their ears. Max and Savannah covered their own ears as they realized that what they had heard was meant for a warning.

Master pulled down on a lever. Max and Savannah staggered as the sold rock beneath their feet jumped. A rolling cloud of dust and debris blew out of the large tunnel directly ahead of the train as a tremendous explosion went off somewhere inside, demolishing the wall that sealed off the tunnel, filling the cavern with choking smoke and dust.

All over Bartertown residents were startled out of stupors or sleep by the sound of distant thunder. Entity froze, midway through a t'ai chi movement, her face suddenly taut with foreboding as her penthouse was shaken by an earth tremor. She turned, heading for her periscope.

"All aboard!" Master cried exultantly. "Platform one! The Orient Express!"

Pig Killer threw the locomotive into gear. With a screech of protest the steaming engine came alive, straining at the shackles of pipe and cable that held it prisoner . . . and gave Bartertown its power. Max and Savannah hurried through the dust, coughing, their eyes running, heading for the train.

High above their heads, Entity shoved the periscope down into viewing position, swiveling it heedlessly through the billowing clouds of dust that were all she could see . . . searching for an explanation.

Master looked up as the periscope dropped, pointing. "It's her!"

Max stopped running and turned back toward the scope while Savannah ran on toward the train. He leaned down, catching up Ironbar Bassey's fallen musket, his face grim. Max stood waiting, staring toward the scope's moving lens until it stopped, pointing directly at him, and he was certain that Entity could see his face.

Entity gasped in disbelief as a dead man looked her in the eye. She jerked back from the viewing slot, leaned forward again, staring through the slot as the warrior she had sent to certain death calmly raised a gun and took aim at her. Max fired, blowing apart the periscope's lense, and she saw nothing more.

Max lowered the musket, his face filled with sour satisfaction, and started on toward the train again.

A heavy, tattooed arm dropped around his neck, jerking him back, throttling him. Max swung up the gun butt, striking blindly behind him, smashing Ironbar's totem face from his back. He jerked free, spinning around, raising the musket. He fired again; heard the hollow click of the hammer on an empty chamber. Ironbar grinned, drawing his machete and raising it high as he started forward. Max began to back away, holding the useless gun in his raised hands to block the blow.

Seeing Max's danger, Scrooloose grabbed hold of a hanging cable, remembering how Mr. Skyfish had come to his own rescue. He swooped down from the train platform toward the two men, just as Savannah, running back, threw herself on Ironbar from behind and sank her teeth into his neck.

Ironbar staggered and fell to his knees with a roar of pain and fury, dragging Savannah down with him as Scrooloose sailed over their heads and crashed dead into Max. Max sprawled on the ground, the wind knocked out of him; he lay gasping and stunned as Ironbar scrambled to his feet again, heaving Savannah from his back, and picked up his machete.

Scrooloose, flailing wildly at the end of his rope, reached the limit of his swing and hurtled back again, straight into Ironbar. Ironbar flew backward, the machete sailing from his hand as he tumbled head over heels into a waiting vat of pigshit.

Scrooloose landed on the train platform with an ungainly thud as Pig Killer opened the throttle up all the way, grinning with delight. Max picked himself up as Savannah hauled on his arm; together they ran back to the train. They scrambled aboard the engine, clinging to its side while the whole train shuddered, its wheels grinding out sparks as it fought to move forward on the track. Max and Savannah looked up as the network of pipes surrounding the train gave way with a squeal of agonized metal and a series of small explosions. Flames and steam belched out into the air as the explosions began to spread. The reek of escaping methane filled the Underworld.

Above ground, the Collector ran frantically toward Entity's penthouse, bursting with news that was already no news to her: A dead man was walking through the Underworld. But as he ran the ground began to shudder beneath his feet; smoke and flames erupted from the vents and chimneys that riddled Bartertown as a chain reaction of explosions spread through the streets. Next to him a pipe exploded and sent him reeling toward a storage shed. The shed went up, pitching him back toward the tavern, which exploded in turn, propelling him on down the street like a pinball. The walking dead man had only been a sign . . . this was the end of the world.

Wheezing asthmatically, he reached Entity's penthouse at last. He looked up, shouting her name, his voice lost in the sound of explosions. Fire was already licking at the base of the tower; the wooden elevator cage was in flames. Entity appeared suddenly on the platform high above, looking out at her city going up in smoke, at the terrified people below running in all directions. She wore studded battle armor, and her face was contorted with fury as she turned away again.

Back in the Underworld Max and Savannah clung precariously to the train's side as it lurched forward like a straining wrestler. Behind them several small faces popped out of the windows of Master's home, staring in wide-eyed wonder as more pipes and cables tore away. The train broke free as a final enormous pipe exploded, and began to move down the tracks at last, gathering speed. Panic-stricken pigs rushed out of its way, squealing in fright. Fire rained down on their heads and roared up through every remaining chimney in the roof of their world, exploding into the open air; the train thundered away into the tunnel, heading for the surface and freedom.

The Underworld was closer to resembling hell than it had ever been before, a sea of billowing fog where broken pipes belched smoke and licking tongues of fire. The train had disappeared and, with it, all signs of human habitation.

Slowly the top of a shaven head emerged from a vat of excrement . . . the eyes, the dripping face of Ironbar Bassey. He gazed in stupefied rage at the destruction around him, the ruins of his kingdom. Climbing out of the vat, he started away through the frantic pigs, heading for the surface and his revenge.

An explosion ripped the base of Entity's penthouse as more burning gases burst through the surface. Flames began to eat their way up the legs of the tower, set it burning like a fuse. The Collector watched helplessly, unable to do anything but scream, "Aunty! Aunty!" in fear and warning.

Inside the penthouse, Entity rummaged through a weapons chest, pulling out a bandolier of bullets and slinging it over her shoulder. She lifted out a machine gun and climbed to her feet as the gauze walls of her tent blazed up, shriveling away like tissue. Beneath her feet the floor began to shudder.

Below the tower Guards and gawkers turned tail and ran for their lives. The Collector screamed in terror, for Entity, and then suddenly, piercingly, for himself. The whole tower was tilting, the penthouse blazing like a torch as it toppled directly toward him.

Entity had a brief, stunned view of the Collector standing below, his upturned face paralyzed with fear as she rode the falling tower down. She leaped free at the final instant, landing facedown on the roof of a tent, her clothes smoldering, her gun still clutched in her fist. She slid down the tentside to the ground as, behind her, the flaming tower fell to earth with a shuddering crash.

Stumbling to her feet, she ran back toward the tower's wreckage, pulled up short as she saw the Collector lying sprawled facedown in the dirt, his body crushed beneath a steel pylon, his face a mask of agony. He reached out to her with a blackened, bloody hand.

She ran forward, kneeled down by his side, dropping her gun. Holding him in her arms, caressing his bald head tenderly, she murmured gentle words as his glazing eyes flickered shut for the last time. She laid his motionless body on the ground again and rose to her feet, picking up her gun. The fires of hell reflected in her eyes as she ran on down the street.

CHAPTER 16

ESCAPE AND PURSUIT

The train steamed upward through the smoke-filled tunnel, still gathering speed. Pig Killer peered ahead, coughing and blinking his eyes, Cusha and Tubba still perched beside him on the seat. Through the smoke and dust he caught a sudden glimpse of two Guards who had started into the tunnel and were running like hell back the way they'd come; their fleeing forms were silhouetted in the widening arc of light that was the tunnel's mouth.

Sunlight broke across Pig Killer's face; he grinned and drew a deep breath of free air at last, as the train roared out of the tunnel and into the light of day for the first time in two decades. The track was still climbing toward the desert above, rising through a narrow cut in the rock; dust from the explosion that had unblocked the tunnel entrance fogged the air.

Four more Imperial Guards stood waiting beside their

vehicles. They froze as the two men burst frantically back out of the gloom, yelling, turned tail at the sight of what was following them, and ran for their lives. They threw themselves aside at the last minute, sprawling in the dirt as the train thundered past them and away into the desert.

The train kept going, leaving behind it a town in ruins and a population in chaos. Flames gutted the wreckage of Bartertown as small pockets as methane continued to explode. Groups of traders and dealers threw together their few salvageable goods, abandoning Bartertown like rats leaving a sinking ship. A herd of pigs, escapees from Underworld, charged through the side alleys around Thunderdome and poured out the entrance tunnel.

Dr. Dealgood left his apartment and his world behind, leading his white horse through the streets. Tweedledum shepherded the four remaining camels, following at his heels; Tweedledummer dragged the handcart laden with weapons, water, and food. Dr. Dealgood shouted at the passersby, selling as he went, never one to pass up an opportunity. "Demolition sale! Everything goes . . . final clearance!" He flinched as an explosion ripped apart a chimney behind him. "Fire sale! Make me an offer. Four camels." Another, bigger explosion shook the ground under his feet; a piece of flying fur smacked him in the face as he turned back, startled. He blinked and shook his head. "One camel!" he shouted, shrugging philosophically. "It won't last—buy now!"

In the center of town the Imperial Guards gathered together what was left of their fleet of armored pursuit vehicles, pulling up in semicircle around Entity as she arrived with the mechanic Blackfinger. Climbing out of her own vehicle, she stood facing the Guards, facing the death and destruction everywhere around them.

"Bartertown lives!" she shouted fiercely. "Tomorrow we rebuild." She held up her rifle, her voice raw, her face alive with fanatical belief. Behind her, Blackfinger tinkered with the engine of her vehicle, hurriedly fine-tuning it for maximum performance.

"I want the little man back. Alive." Entity turned, looking from one Guard to another, marking the brutal, determined faces and the arsenal of crossbows, guns, chains, knives and clubs that surrounded her, all at her command. "And for those who took him—no mercy." The Guards cheered and started their engines. She climbed into her own vehicle again, not bothering to say what would happen if no one brought him back. Master was the key to everything; if they didn't get him back, there would be no rebuilding.

The air was filled with the roar of revving motors, the click of weapons being checked and loaded. Entity put her foot down on the accelerator. Her car roared out of the square, leading the pack of vengeful pursuers toward the tunnel and the desert beyond.

And Blackfinger, who had slid under her car to make a final adjustment, swore in surprise as the superstructure above him suddenly pulled away. Instinctively he reached up, grabbing hold of the fender, damned if he was going to be left behind. He hung on like a leech, riding the rollerboard strapped to his back as the vehicle shot away down the street.

Until the car hit a pothole filled with water. Blackfinger plunged into the soup, losing his handhold. Abandoned, dripping mud and water, he watched as Aunty's army streamed past around him, following her out into the desert.

Furious and disgusted, he leaped to his feet and ran after them, searching desperately for any transportation that was still in town. Ahead of him Dr. Dealgood was leading the white horse. Blackfinger scrambled up a ladder, ran out along the ledge at the front of the Palace of Dreams, and leaped onto the horse's back.

Dr. Dealgood looked up, astounded, as Blackfinger landed on his horse. The frightened horse reared in surprise and lunged sideways. Blackfinger slid from its back, half falling, half surrendering, realizing he knew everything about cars and nothing whatsoever about animals. Dr. Dealgood jerked the horse forward with a curse, hurrying on his way.

Swearing a black streak, Blackfinger climbed back onto the ledge as Tweedledum passed, leading the last camel. He leaped onto the camel's back. The camel sat down in the street with a grunt of outrage. Blackfinger slid off again, defeated, and raced on toward the gate.

An enormous armored attack vehicle—the one Blackfinger had fondly dubbed Big Foot—came charging down the street behind him. Blackfinger leaped onto a barrel as it passed, threw himself on board as it slewed by. He hauled himself up onto its rear end, hanging on, and gave an exultant rebel yell.

Out on the desert the train steamed on across the empty plateau, trailing pipes and wreckage. Pig Killer was still at the wheel with the two kids beside him, the wind whipping their hair as they hung out the window, watching the landscape pass with delight and wonder.

Max climbed forward along the side of the engine until he reached the window on Pig Killer's side of the car. "So, what's the plan?" he shouted.

"Plan?" Pig Killer shrugged, still grinning, living for the moment. "There ain't no plan."

Max frowned. Master had gotten them all out of

Bartertown alive, something Max could still hardly believe. . . . He must have had something more in mind. There was no sign of pursuit yet, but there would be— and this train hadn't been built for speed. Their trouble wasn't over yet. "Where are we going?"

Pig Killer looked ahead again. "The end of the track," he said good-naturedly.

"Where's that?"

Pig Killer laughed. "Who knows?"

Max turned away from the window with a grimace, signaling to Savannah with a jerk of his head. Together they began to inch back toward Master's house on the flatbed car behind them.

Inside his former home, Master stood packing his valuables into a battered satchel, preparing for the moment when they would have to abandon the train. He had no idea how far this line ran now or how far the train would get before its fuel ran out. But he had no illusions about what they would find at the end of the track. Around him Mr. Skyfish, Anna Goanna, Eddie, and Scrooloose poked and prodded at the mind-boggling array of mementos he had collected over the years. He felt surprisingly happy, in spite of their uncertain future—he was free, and he was surrounded by children, which made him think of Blaster.

Master took down a picture of Blaster, a few favorite books, and his drafting equipment, dropped them into his satchel without looking back . . . not noticing that Scrooloose repeated his every move in reverse, pulling each thing out again as he put it in, examining it minutely.

Master dropped in a handful of pencils, turning away again. Scrooloose retrieved them, studied them, stuffed one into his mouth, and bit it in half, chewing experimentally.

Anna Goanna stood beside an ancient hand-cranked gramophone, winding its handle. Nothing happened. Disappointed but still curious, she peered underneath it, then into its horn. Eddie turned away from her, getting restless. He moved back to stand beside Scrooloose, who offered him a pencil. Eddie stuck it into his mouth and bit down as Scrooloose looked into Master's bag again. Pulling out a splayed toothbrush, he stared at it and grinned with sudden inspiration. Raising his hand, he began to brush his hair.

Anna discovered the gramophone's dust cover and raised it, jerked back in surprise. A record was revolving slowly on its turntable. She grabbed Mr. Skyfish's arm, pointing at it wide-eyed, whispering, "He's got his own sonic." Reaching into the folds of her clothing, she pulled out the record that was her legacy from Gekko.

Mr. Skyfish took the battered record from her, turning it over in his hands, staring at the revolving turntable. "Gekko had it straight," he murmured with mingled amazement and sorrow. "It ain't bullshit." Maybe one day his own dream would even come true. He set the record on top of the one already resting on the turntable.

Anna began to crank the handle; the record began to spin again, faster and faster. They pushed their faces up close to the horn, listening. But still there was no sound from it. Behind them, Scrooloose retrieved a pair of binoculars from the satchel and raised them to his eyes. He peered through the wrong end, lowered them again, unimpressed by the results.

Max stood in the doorway of the carriage, watching in silence, a strange play of expressions passing over his face. He stepped aside again, out of their sight, as Anna and Skyfish began to recite, "Delta-Fox-X-ray" in eager unison.

Standing on the platform outside the house, Max reached in through the open window beside them and dropped the gramophone's needle onto the record. The static crackle and pop of the record's badly scratched surface echoed from the gramophone's speaker horn. Scrooloose dropped the binoculars and crowded in beside Anna and Mr. Skyfish as Max turned up the gramophone's volume. Behind them Eddie stooped over to pick up the lenses as the others pressed their ears closer to the horn.

A woman's voice began to recite, very precisely, "Repeat after me: *Bonjour, monsieur . . . comment allez-vous*? Good morning. How are you?"

"Bonjour!" Anna and Mr. Skyfish repeated obediently. "Good morning! How are you?"

"Ou allez vous?" the voice said. "Where are you going?"

They echoed the words again.

"Je vais chez mois. I am going home."

"Je vais chez mois," they murmured reverently. "I am going home . . . ."

Max's mouth stretched into a wry smile as he listened and watched. Savannah stood beside him smiling too as she watched the awestricken faces of her friends and heard the message they were being given by the disembodied voice. Behind them, Eddie wandered away toward the back of the house, peering out the rear window. He giggled with delight as he discovered the end of the glasses that worked.

Looking out the window and down the tracks behind them, he discovered a hand-powered rail cart. Pumping furiously up and down on its handle was Ironbar Bassey, gaining on the train with maniacal determination. Eddie laughed out loud as he watched . . . screamed suddenly as the enormous, snarling face of a monster filled his view.

The Guard smashed his way in through the window, knocking Eddie sprawling as he lunged after Master. The Tribe scattered in fright as his hand closed over Master's collar, dragging the small man toward the window.

Max caught up a frying pan from Master's stove and swung it, smashing the Guard in the head, knocking him back and out as a second Guard burst in through the window on the far side of the carriage. Scrooloose grabbed up a pot and walloped him in turn.

Max grinned; the kids laughed with wild triumph . . . their faces changed as another Guard's arm locked around his neck, wrenching him away from the window.

Max lost his grip on the sill and his balance with it, falling out and away from the train with the Guard still hanging on to him. Together they crashed down with jarring force onto the rear end of a pursuit vehicle tracking beside the train. Max drove an elbow into the Guard's ribs, breaking his stranglehold as they slid down the fender toward the wheels. Clawing for a handhold, he locked his arms through the framework that held the car's methane tanks and hung on with all his strength.

The Guard slipped farther, hanging on to the back of Max's jacket, dragging him down. Clinging to the framework, his muscles straining, Max let one arm, and then the other, slip out of his sleeves . . . lashed out viciously with his feet. The Guard fell away under the wheels with a scream.

Blinking the sweat and dust out of his eyes, Max looked toward the train, saw the kids hanging out the windows staring back at him, Savannah clinging to the side of Master's house with her knife in her fist. The rest of Entity's pursuit vehicles were swarming around the train like ants after honey; they were out of the calm eye and back in the full fury of the storm again.

Max hauled himself up over the vehicle's rawhide-covered rear end, clambering forward toward the driver. He pulled himself up over the lip of the car's open cockpit just as the driver looked up; Max drove his fist into the Guard's upturned face. The car lurched and veered away from the train, careening out of control as Max hauled the unconscious driver aside and dropped down into his seat.

Back on the train, the Tribe still stood at the window, watching in awe as Max brought the car back under control, heading back toward the train . . . all except Scrooloose. Scrooloose climbed lithely up onto the balcony at the front of the little house, frying pan in hand. He grinned as what had once been Max's own dune buggy drew up even with the train. He crouched and leaped. . . .

Scrooloose landed on the rear of the buggy, still clutching the frying pan. Anna Goanna, Mr. Skyfish, and Eddie turned back in amazement, rushing to the other side of the train to watch Scrooloose as he scrambled toward the front of the vehicle.

Squatting on the framework of bars directly above the driver, Scrooloose waited for him to look up and brought the frying pan down on his head with a ringing thud. The driver slumped over the wheel, his foot still jammed down on the accelerator. Scrooloose hung on, settling back with a grin of triumph to enjoy the ride.

Pig Killer, Tubba, and Cusha looked out the window of the locomotive's cab, their jaws dropping as Scrooloose roared past them and on ahead, riding on the wildly out of control pursuit vehicle. Pig Killer grimaced in horror as the buggy veered suddenly, plunging up the embankment and onto the tracks in front of the hurtling train. He looked down frantically, searching for the brake; looked up again and shut his eyes as Scrooloose's vehicle leaped the tracks like a jackrabbit. The train flew on, missing its tail end by inches.

Pig Killer opened his eyes as no sickening impact jarred through him; slowly Cusha and Tubba did the same. They turned together, looking out the window on the far side of the cab, watching Scrooloose's vehicle bounce away down the embankment and blast off across the desert.

Still clinging to the car's roof, Scrooloose looked down and saw the driver starting to stir. Raising his frying pan, Scrooloose let him have it again. The Guard slumped obediently over the wheel. Scrooloose looked out and around him, watching the other cars. There was obviously something to this process that he was missing. . . . He picked up his frying pan. Holding it in front of him, he began to steer, still watching the other drivers. He grinned, sure that he had found the sympathetic magic that controlled his rampaging vehicle.

Behind the train, a snarling Ironbar Bassey was still following, pumping the handcar with furious obsession but slowly falling behind. He looked over as another wave of pursuers pulled even with him. One of the drivers, spotting him, veered up onto the embankment and accelerated to run parallel.

Ironbar let go of the car and leaped, abandoning the handcar for one that could give him what he needed. He landed on the armored cage on top of the other vehicle, steadied himself, bellowed orders at the driver. The Guard bounced back onto the flat, speeding up until he was running alongside a second vehicle. Ironbar leaped again, from the roof of his own car to the next one, already scrambling across the second vehicle's rear end as he bellowed another command. The second driver matched speeds with a third car, this one mounted with a spring-loaded heavy-duty harpoon gun. Ironbar sprang from car to car once more, miscalculated the leap this time, and lost his balance as he landed. Tumbling down over its side, he hooked a hold on the nest of tanks and snarled hoses with a muscle-wrenching effort, his steel-shod boots dragging in the dirt, kicking up sparks. He hauled himself back aboard; the driver gunned the engine as Ironbar scrambled into position behind the harpoon, murder in his eyes.

The harpoon vehicle charged up through the marauder pack, gaining fast on the locomotive. Passing the flatbed car like a cruising shark, it drew even with the engine. Pig Killer looked out the window at the sound of it pulling up alongside. His face fell as he saw Ironbar Bassey swiveling the gun toward the train with the grinning anticipation of Ahab. His hands tightened on the wheel as he saw the weapon, the harpoon shaft as thick as his wrist, the gleaming steel barb at its tip circling toward him. He watched Ironbar take aim with horrified fascination.

Ironbar fired. The harpoon smashed into the door of the cab with a shuddering impact. Pig Killer grinned in astonished relief . . . his eyes glazed, and he slumped against the door, unconscious. Cusha turned in sudden fright, looking down to see the harpoon's dripping point buried in his thigh, pinning him to the cab door. Calmly Ironbar reloaded and recocked his weapon as the driver swung closer to the train, coming in for the kill.

Max pushed his commandeered vehicle to its limit as Savannah signaled frantically from the roof of Master's house. Aiming for the tracks at top speed, he ramped up the embankment. The car sailed into the air, slammed down on the other side with a spine-jarring impact. Max accelerated again, hurtling toward the vehicle ahead. Every sense was heightened, his nerves singing like electric wires with an intensity that he only felt at a moment like this . . . behind the wheel of a speeding car, on the tight wire between life and death. The merciless concentration that had made him the best pursuit driver on the Main Force Patrol took him by the throat as he saw the harpoon gun and who was riding it.

Max skidded into position behind the harpoon vehicle, bumper to bumper, and stepped on the accelerator again. He rammed the car ahead with a grinding crunch of metal.

The harpoon vehicle lurched crazily with the impact. Ironbar pitched forward over the gun, losing his shot. Gritting his teeth, Max slammed into the car again, harder this time, driving it on past the locomotive's cab, ruining Ironbar's line of fire . . . rammed it again and again, shunting it forward of the train. Veering to the right, he slammed into its rear end one final time, driving it up the embankment and onto the tracks.

The engine hurtled toward the stranded car. Ironbar struggled upright, dazed, swiveling his head. His eyes bulged; he screamed. The driverless train smashed into the harpoon vehicle, obliterating it. Pieces of car flew into the air and rained down over Max's vehicle, over the engine roaring on down the track.

Still pacing the train, Max looked across and stared in disbelief. Clinging to the front of the locomotive, looking like a slab of charred meat but still alive, was Ironbar Bassey. That son of a bitch had more lives than a cockroach.

Max stayed even with the engine, groping beside him on the seat for the Guard's shotgun . . . twisted and looked back over his shoulder as he heard another vehicle closing with his own. The pack had laid off him until now, not realizing that he wasn't one of their own, but what he had just done to Bassey had blown his cover all to hell, along with the harpoon car.

Max swore under his breath. Bearing down on him now was the monster called Big Foot—a vehicle the size of a diesel truck and just as powerful, its front end reinforced with steel plates. Max floored the accelerator of his own car, but Big Foot surged forward, cresting over him like a tidal wave. Big Foot rammed Max's vehicle with brutal force; Max's head cracked against the back of the cockpit. He clung to the steering wheel with white-knuckled hands, trying to keep control as Big Foot shunted him again.

His car veered wildly, swerving out of control, careening away across the desert at right angles to the train. Big Foot let him go, pulling back toward the train after better prey. A Guard scrambled out of the vehicle's cab onto its roof, clung there precariously, and leaped across to the train. Big Foot pulled on ahead, giving way to Aunty Entity's own car coming up through the pack, closing in on the train and its precious cargo.

With a wrenching effort Max got his car under control again, fishtailed around and headed back toward the locomotive at top speed, gaining fast on the train and Entity. Up ahead, the kids were no longer in sight as Entity transferred from her vehicle to the side of the house, helped on board by the waiting Guard. As Max watched, Entity's vehicle accelerated forward again, letting Blackfinger clamber on board the train at the point where the flatbed car was coupled to the locomotive. If he uncoupled the car from the engine, that was the end of it. Master would be a sitting duck and the kids as good as dead. He knew what Entity was after—what they were all after—now. Master. Even revenge came second to getting Master back; without Master there was no Bartertown. But he had nearly paid for Master's life with his own once already, and he was damned if Entity was taking the little man back . . . or getting any satisfaction, either.

Entity's Guard lunged through the side window of the little house; inside, waiting for him, Mr. Skyfish clouted him with his ax. Entity pushed her way in at the rear, grabbing for Master. Eddie picked up a pan and bashed her, knocking her back out the window.

Max drove his vehicle up onto the tracks, straddling the rails, tailgating the train. He saw Entity tumble backwards as she lost her grip; she clung desperately to the superstructure of Master's house, barely saving herself from falling beneath his wheels. Slowly, painfully, she pulled herself up onto the platform again while up above her the Guard worked his way forward along the side of the house, disappearing from Max's view.

Inside the house the kids and Master spun around, their muscles tensing as the Guard tried the handle of the door. It was locked; the motion stopped. Their faces eased.

The door burst inward with an earsplitting crash as the Guard kicked it off its hinges. He burst through, his spined and armored bulk filling the small room as he started for Master.

Suddenly he was yanked backwards; a hammer thudded down on his head, and he sprawled to the floor. Savannah stood in the doorway, motioning frantically. "C'mon!" She hurried Master and the others out onto the balcony, looking down at Blackfinger working below to pry loose the coupling pin. Guided and pushed by Savannah, Anna Goanna and then Eddie made the leap across the house to the engine. Blackfinger looked up, swore in frustration as he saw them leap past overhead.

Entity inched her way along the side of the flatbed, matching his curses with her own as she saw the children make the leap to the engine. But as she reached the front of the house she saw Master, still aboard on her side. "Pull the pin!" she shouted.

Blackfinger jerked out the pin; the flatbed car began to slow imperceptibly, drifting away from the locomotive.

Savannah caught Master up in her arms as she heard Entity's shout. Darting forward, she made the leap across onto the engine; the others reached out for her as she landed, dragging them both aboard. "Hold it!" Entity screamed, too late.

Blackfinger, crouched on the front of the flatbed car, looked up, down again, to where nearly a yard separated car and engine already. Grimly he threw himself forward, catching hold of the locomotive's rear end. His feet slid along the flatbed, caught on a bar attached to the front of Master's house, jerking his forward motion to a stop. Hanging on with all his strength to the rear of the locomotive, he became a human coupler. Gritting his teeth, he swore to himself that the reward had better be worth it. . . .

Entity scrambled up onto the balcony. Reaching across with single-minded ferocity, she grabbed Master by the leg. Balanced precariously on the back of the engine, Savannah held him tighter, baring her teeth in defiance; pulling back as Entity tried to jerk Master from her arms. Entity yanked harder, her own position secure;

Savannah felt the one sweating hand with which she clung to a broken steampipe begin to slip. . . .

Entity yanked again, jerking Savannah's hand loose from the pipe. Pitching forward, Savannah let go of Master, barely managing to save herself from falling off the train as he swung helplessly across the gap and into Entity's grasp.

"Let go!" Entity shouted.

Blackfinger let go with supreme gratitude . . . fell, arms flailing, almost under the wheels of the carriage. But his feet held on the bar; he twisted like a panic-stricken acrobat, managed to drag himself back on board before the tracks turned him into hamburger.

Entity held Master up in her arms, waving him like a trophy for her Guards to see, her eyes shining with wild triumph. Savannah and the Tribe looked back in dismay as the engine slowly pulled away from the carriage again. Then all at once Savannah's face changed. Master, held high in Entity's arms, twisted to look behind him as he saw the expression on her face.

Behind Entity, Max pulled himself up the rear of the little house. Getting his feet under him, he came forward along the roof, running hard, as the gap between car and train slowly widened.

Master held up his arms. . . .

Max reached the front of the car, scooped Master out of Entity's hands without missing a step, and leaped across the gap.

Half a dozen reaching hands hauled them aboard the locomotive. Max looked back, panting, wiping his face with his arm; saw Entity gaping in stunned fury as the locomotive, with all of the Tribe, Max, and Master clinging to its sides, pulled away from her once more.

Max sighed, pushing Master farther up onto the back

of the engine, scrambling up beside him to a more secure perch. Everyone was safely on board, and for the moment there were no unwanted visitors.

Except the one he had forgotten, still clinging like a squashed beetle to the front of the locomotive. Dodging the weapons and pieces of junk hurled at him from the cab, Ironbar Bassey hauled himself up and over the mutant locomotive's truck shell, working his way back toward the group of refugees riding precariously on its spine. Inching his way along an exposed pipe, he lunged upward, grabbing Master by the foot. Half a dozen small hands and feet began to kick and punch him; he ignored the blows, his eyes fixed with maniacal obsession on his prey, hauling Master down with inexorable power. With a cry Master lost his handhold and began to fall.

Max's heavy boot crashed into the side of Ironbar's bloody, smoke-blackened head. Ironbar lost his grip on Master as the pipe he clung to gave way, swinging out at right angles to the train, leaving him dangling in midair with the ground rushing past in a sickening blur below.

A rider on a motorcycle pulled up alongside the embankment, holding even with Ironbar's dangling body, trying to position his sidecar so that Ironbar could drop into it. "Jump!" he shouted. "Jump!"

Ironbar looked down at the bike rider, gauging his chances, just as the other man looked away again. The rider screamed, slamming on his brakes, as the ground ahead of him suddenly disappeared.

Ironbar's own eyes widened. Just ahead the railroad track crossed a steep gully on a bridge . . . and all along the bridge's length were a series of steel supports rising in his path like hurdles.

The bike rider hit the edge of the gully, still braking hard but not hard enough. The nose of his bike dropped out from under him as it went over the edge, catapulting him out into the air.

Ironbar watched him fall; looked up again and saw the first of the steel supports coming at him like a club. With a herculean effort he swung himself up, hiking his feet agonizingly over the first hurdle ... the second ... then the third ... the fourth ... the last.

They were on the other side of the bridge. Wheezing for breath, he grinned in triumph, looking back at the locomotive. One of the snot-nosed kids was perched over the other end of the pipe, holding an ax, banging away at it with all his strength. Ironbar watched the pipe begin to give way, his smile of satisfaction turning sick.

The pipe broke, dumping Ironbar's body into the cinders at the side of the track. He hit and rolled, disappearing into the dust as the train steamed on around the bend.

Max and Savannah climbed down from the engine's back and scrambled forward to the cab door. Pig Killer, conscious again and propped up in the driver's seat, looked out at Max with a feeble grin. Max looked down at the harpoon shaft protruding from the door, looked in through the window at the damage it had done. Taking a deep breath, he said, "I'm gonna open the door. I'll count to three."

Pig Killer nodded weakly.

"One ..." Max said. Pig Killer echoed his count.

Max yanked the door open before Pig Killer had the time to think about it, wrenching the harpoon out of his leg. Pig Killer's eyes glazed with pain; he slumped sideways, close to passing out again.

Behind Max, Savannah reached forward, clutching his shoulder, pointing ahead in sudden fear. Max looked up; his breath caught. He swung into the cab, shoving Pig

Killer aside as he jammed on the brake. Up ahead of them now was . . . nothing.

They had reached the end of the line.

CHAPTER 17

THE END OF THE LINE

The train squealed to a halt in a shower of sparks, groaning in protest, with everyone on board gaping ahead now. The tracks stopped in the middle of nowhere and totally disappeared; a funeral mound of dirt and rubble marked the dead end of their trip. Not far beyond was the sheer drop-off of the mesa's edge; there was no sign at all that the tracks had ever gone any farther. But sitting on the mound of rubble, brandishing a massive rifle, was a young boy in a pith helmet. He held his ground as the train came to a halt less than five feet in front of him; calmly aimed his rifle at the staring faces inside the cab.

Max climbed down, the others piling off the train behind him, ready for a confrontation. Savannah helped Pig Killer from the cab as Max stood glaring at the pint-size hijacker with grim impatience.

"Stick 'em up," the kid said arrogantly. "Or dead

meat." Before they could even respond, the boy suddenly looked past them, his mouth dropping open. "Oh . . . shit," he muttered, "we're all dead meat!" He dropped the rifle and ran. Scrambling like a mountain goat, he disappeared over the edge of the cliff.

Max looked over his shoulder, saw the rising, spreading cloud of dust behind them—Aunty Entity and her army, far behind but coming fast.

Max shouted at the Tribe to follow and took off after the fleeing hijacker. The kid must have come from somewhere, and right now, anywhere had to be better than this.

By the time Entity and her marauders reached the end of the track, the fugitives were only a cloud of dust on a distant mesa top, with the wide floor of a canyon between their fleeing bodies and her revenge. She slammed on her brakes as she saw the edge of the precipice ahead; heard the other vehicles scream to a halt behind her. She sat staring out across the plain. There was no bridge this time, no way for her vehicles to reach the canyon floor safely. Her fists clenched on the steering wheel.

She twisted in her seat at the sound of another vehicle coming up from behind, the driver making no move at all to brake as he neared the cliff. As she watched incredulously, what had once been Max's dune buggy blasted through the gathered Guards and past her like a bat out of hell. The buggy showered her with gravel and dust as it shot off the edge of the cliff, driving straight down the mesa's side. She stared in disbelief at the kamikaze courage of the maniac who was driving it.

She watched him bounce and slew down the mesa wall . . . and land right-side-up at the bottom, gunning away across the flat canyon floor after the distant fugitives. Her disbelief crystalized into resolution. That sonofabitch had guts, but no more than she did. If he could make it, they could all make it. . . . She hadn't lost Master yet. Stamping hard on her accelerator, she drove forward over the edge, and the Guards followed her in a mass.

Down below on the plane, Scrooloose sat behind the wheel of the dune buggy, roaring on toward the distant mesa, his eyes popping, his mouth hanging open, terrified and completely out of control.

Up on the mesa top the kid hijacker was gaining ground on his pursuers, but Max could still make him out up ahead; on the flat mesa top there was nowhere to hide.

Abruptly the kid disappeared. Max sprinted forward, leaving Savannah and the others to help Pig Killer and Master. He ran until he reached the spot where the boy had suddenly ceased to exist. A shaft wide enough for a man opened downward into the mesa; the rungs of a ladder led down into the darkness below. That was where the kid had disappeared to. Something must be down there. . . . Right now Max didn't even care what it was. He scrambled down the ladder, hearing the others follow behind him.

Landing on his feet in a dimly lit tunnel, Max blinked his sun-dazzled eyes until he could see in the gloom and started off in the direction of the kid's retreating footsteps. The Tribe straggled after him, one by one. Room after room hewn out of the rock opened off of the corridor, all of them empty . . . until finally Max reached the one that was not.

The kid bolted on through a door at the other end, leaving Max confronted by a perfectly normal-looking bedroom with a double bed sitting against a side wall.

Someone was lying in bed in calm repose, reading, their face obscured by the full-color cover of an ancient magazine. Max slid to a stop, staring at the startling blues and greens of a tropical island paradise and, in large red letters, the title, DREAM VACATIONS.

Slowly the hands that held the magazine lowered, revealing a face framed by a pith helmet like the kid's and Coke-bottle-bottom glasses. Jedediah stared back at Max in incredulous astonishment.

"You!" Max gasped in equal disbelief, face-to-face at last with the sole cause of all his troubles. His fists clenched. Behind him Savannah and the others began to stumble into the room. Their curious stares mirrored dimly in the shining aluminum headboard of Jedediah's bed.

A guilty grin spread over Jedediah's narrow, equine features. "Me?" he quavered, mentally riffling the files of his past and recent sins; wondering why the man from Thunderdome was standing here in his own bedroom like the Ghost of Errors Past, looking at him with an expression that suggested bloody murder.

Max started toward him with grim inevitability, his hands flexing. "It's your lucky day. . . ."

"It is?" Jedediah asked, not feeling at all blessed by fortune.

"You've got a plane. . . ." Max said, still coming.

"I have—. . ." Jedediah nodded, his panic-stricken mind trying frantically to remember whether he really did or not. Max reached his bedside.

Max grabbed him, jerking him up by the trailing ends of his aviator's scarf until the two men were eyeball to eyeball. "It just might save your life."

"It will!" Jedediah gasped as Max dragged him out of bed and shoved him toward the door.

Jedediah led Max and the others on down the hallway. A growing circle of light grew visible ahead, marking an exit; from somewhere outside Max heard the sweet sound of an airplane engine kicking over.

They emerged into the glaring light of day; glancing up and back, Max saw that the house was actually a honeycomb built into the side of a rocky outcrop, secure and virtually undetectable. He looked ahead again as the others emerged from the doorway into the courtyard.

Sitting in the middle of the yard while Jedediah, Jr. revved up its engine, was the airplane. Its bizarre piece-meal hull shone in the sun, its framework shuddered with the power of its engine. It was suddenly the most beautiful thing he'd ever seen. Max herded kids, adults, and monkey toward the plane and began shoving them into its cramped interior.

"Skyrafter!" Mr. Skyfish cried, dancing with wonder, hanging back to stare at the plane.

Max grabbed him by the arm, cramming him aboard. "Let's go."

"We got the wind up our ass!" Mr. Skyfish yelled exultantly.

Max leaped up into the doorway, bracing himself against the wing strut, half in and half out, as the others squirmed and resettled, trying to make more room.

The plane began to move, lumbering out of the court-yard like a pregnant pelican, taxiing out onto the flat plateau that served as Jedediah's airstrip.

For a long moment the courtyard sat empty and silent, the dust circling slowly, settling from the air. And then the sound of more approaching engines shattered its quiet.

Entity and the Guards who had survived the plunge over the cliff poured down the rocky slopes that flanked

Jedediah's house, into the courtyard below; roared on through the yard without stopping and out onto the field.

Still far ahead of the pack, Scrooloose gunned his motor, driving confidently at last, having finally mastered the controls. He glanced over as the driver stirred on the seat; lifted his frying pan nonchalantly, and splanged the Guard again. He drove on across the plateau, pursuing the dust cloud out ahead with eager incomprehension.

In the plane up ahead Max fought his way forward through the mass of bodies behind Jedediah. It seemed like they had been taxiing for hours. "C'mon!" he shouted, his face lined with tension. "Take it up."

Jedediah shrugged helplessly, fiddling with a chestful of instruments like a nervous priest counting rosary beads. "There's no lift! We've got too much weight."

Max turned back, stumbling over a battered suitcase, realizing that the plane was crammed as full of Jedediah's salvaged junk as it was with people. He picked up the suitcase and hurled it out the open door. "Get this crap out of here!" he shouted. "Everything!" Savannah scrambled to her feet as the others began to look around them for useless ballast. Max and Savannah pitched blankets, cartons, a rusted typewriter, a kitchen sink, even Eddie's teddy bear out the doorway, looking back for signs of pursuit as the trail of jetsam bounced away into the dust.

Max pushed forward again expectantly, looking out through the windshield for open sky. Instead he saw Jedediah go goggle-eyed with horror as Jedediah, Jr. slammed on the brakes. The plane skidded to a halt at the end of the runway . . . the end of the mesa.

Max stared out and down over the edge of the drop-off, swearing, and turned back suddenly at the sound of a vehicle approaching. As he watched it slid into a screeching handbrake U-turn at the edge of the cliff. "Jesus Christ!" It was his own dune buggy, and Scrooloose was driving it. Max leaped out of the plane, Savannah racing after him as he ran to the buggy and hauled Scrooloose out. The plane was already turning around at the brink of the mesa as they dragged him bodily back to it.

Max jammed Scrooloose and Savannah into the plane, which was now facing back the way it had come. He started to climb in.

Abruptly the engine died. Max spun around, his eyes cold with fury, to see Jedediah and Jedediah, Jr. scramble down from the cockpit. Man and boy stood side by side, staring away across the plain. Jedediah raised an arcane set of opera glasses, peering through them like a distressed playgoer. Perfectly visible even to his naked eyes, Max saw what Jedediah was looking at—the dust cloud approaching like a storm across the plain, below it the vehicles of Entity's army racing toward them for the kill.

Max ran forward as Jedediah pulled a white handkerchief from his pocket and began to wave it, abandoning the plane, lurching toward the approaching storm. "We're friendly! We're friendly! All men are brothers," Jedediah quavered. His lips pulled back from his long white teeth in a tremulous grin of appeasement, his long arm wrapped convulsively around his son's shoulders.

Max caught hold of Jedediah, pushing him back toward the plane. "Start her up!"

Jedediah fiddled infuriatingly with the pile of junk hanging around his neck, still grinning like a jackass as he mumbled nervously, "You might not understand this—it's very technical—but we haven't got a chance." He peered at Max with the expression of a man trying to explain aerodynamics to an irate gorilla. "There's not enough runway." He waved his arm, looking back toward the approach of Doom, his face as white as a sheet.

Max's fists tightened on his scarf, twisting. "There will be," he murmured, his voice soft and deadly. He shoved Jedediah back toward the plane. Savannah and Pig Killed stood waiting, knives drawn, by the cabin door.

"Yes . . . yes . . ." Jedediah gibbered, scurrying back to the cockpit with his son in tow, "of course there will be." He disappeared inside; the engine sputtered once and caught, the propeller came alive and faded into a blur of motion. From inside the plane Max heard voices calling to him.

He looked ahead again, his mouth pressed tight, watching the first wave of Aunty's Guards close in. Then he turned and ran toward his waiting buggy.

Entity accelerated toward the distant airplane, seeing its nose turned to face them like a beast at bay. This time the rats had nowhere left to run. She glanced aside as a vehicle thundered past her, saw Ironbar Bassey weaving his way though the pack toward the lead, his blackened, bloody face set in an animal's snarl.

Up ahead the plane suddenly started forward, running to meet them like a suicidal pigeon. As Entity watched it come, frowning with surprise, she suddenly saw another vehicle emerge from the dust behind it and draw even with the plane . . . one of her own vehicles. *Who the bloody hell was driving that thing, and what the hell was he doing?* And suddenly she knew.

Max gunned the engine, pulling abreast of the plane, amazed at how much power his own vehicle had, souped up and running on methane. He glanced toward the cockpit. Jedediah looked back at him with mingled panic and desperation, looked ahead again at the oncoming wall of death. Max pulled even with the plane's open doorway, saw Savannah and Pig Killer looking out at him; saw in their eyes for one brief second something far more profound than gratitude. He raised his hand in farewell, looked ahead again, jamming the accelerator down to the floor.

Savannah and Pig Killer watched as the dune buggy surged out ahead of the lumbering plane; with no words for what they felt, no time left to speak them . . .

Max left the plane behind, outdistancing it with ease as it fought to reach airspeed. Up ahead now, he began to make out detail on individual vehicles. He picked out Entity's, saw one car pull out ahead of the rest, realized that it was Ironbar Bassey bearing down on him, leading the pack, hell-bent on vengeance.

Max smiled. If there was one person in the approaching mass of metal and flesh that he could take with him into hell, Ironbar was the one he would have chosen. And he knew that Bassey wanted it just as much as he did. Ironbar would hold to this collision course if it killed him . . . and that was just what he needed.

He was alone; he had never felt more alone in his life, or more alive. Fear was screaming somewhere deep inside him, held captive behind the bars of his will, as he was held inside this cage of metal. It had always been that way, when he had been a Bronze, hurtling down the road toward what could be his own death coming straight at him. It was fear that gave him the razor's edge; that honed every movement, that set his mind free and his nerves on fire, that slowed time. . . .

Max reached out, caught hold of the Guard lying dead or unconscious on the seat beside him. Dragging the body toward the driver's seat, he shoved it into position, jamming the Guard's foot down on the accelerator. He had one chance left to survive this . . . a snowball's chance in hell, but he had to take it. With the car still moving at top speed, still steering it, Max pulled himself up and out of the window, clambered up onto the side of the buggy. Crouching there, the fingers of one hand locked over the steering wheel, his heart hammering against his ribs, he watched Ironbar's vehicle bear down on him, growing larger and larger until it seemed to fill the world . . . until he could see Ironbar's face, contorted with rage. . . . He jumped.

The two vehicles smashed headlong into each other with a sound like the end of the world. Max was catapulting through space. . . .

Time seemed to stop. For an endless moment he was flying, weightless, while below him pieces of his car and Ironbar's rained down like shrapnel. The vehicles following hard behind Ironbar's swerved, too late, screeching, rolling, crashing into the wreckage below. The mass of twisted metal went up in a fireball as fuel from smashed tanks ignited. Jedediah's plane gained critical momentum at the last possible moment. With a final, jarring bounce, its wheels left the ground for good, and it staggered into the air.

For a split second Max glimpsed the plane, airborne at last, its wheels just clearing the flaming wreckage as it rose into the sky. And then gravity reclaimed him; time began to flow again. . . . The ground rushed up to meet him with terrifying speed.

Jedediah and his son stared down at the fireball below, their faces frozen in a rictus smile of disbelief. Behind them Savannah, Pig Killer, and the children hung out of the doorway, looking down as the plane soared higher into the air, leaving Max behind. Beside Savannah, Master watched in silence, seeing Entity staring after him, powerless at last, as he was . . . as Bartertown was.

Entity slowed her vehicle as she watched the plane bank away from her, rising like a phoenix, already beyond her reach forever, growing smaller and smaller in the infinite reaches of the sky... taking Master away from her, and with him all hope she had had of rebuilding her city. She slammed on the brake as the flaming wreckage, Ironbar Bassey's funeral pyre, rose up before her.

Around her the Guards who had managed to avoid the crash pulled up in a semicircle, waiting for further orders. She stopped her own vehicle and climbed out; the two Guards riding with her followed, flanking her, their weapons ready. Slowly she crossed the space of ground that separated her from the place where Max lay sprawled in the dirt. Behind him the air was filled with smoke, the ground littered with wreckage—tires, twisted metal, broken glass.

She stopped, looking down at his motionless body, her face clenched. Beside her the Guards cocked their crossbows, preparing to make certain that he would never get up again.

Max stirred, raising his head with a painful effort at the sound of weapons being readied. So he was still alive.... His clothing was in rags, his face was smeared with blood and dirt until he was almost unrecognizable. But she knew those eyes... she would never forget those eyes.

The Guards raised their weapons, taking aim. Max stared up at them with bleak resignation, too beaten to resist.

Entity watched his face, raised her hands abruptly, forcing the Guards' weapons down. She stared at Max again through an endless moment. "Ain't we a pair, raggedy-man," she said softly.

Max stared up at her, his face filling with dazed

incomprehension. She smiled and turned on her heel, striding back toward her vehicle. The Guards followed her, unquestioning.

As she reached the driver's seat Entity paused, turned back for one last look at the man who had single-handedly brought to ruin everything that she had struggled for so long to build and sweated blood to hold together . . . because, in the end, he had been truer to the Law that she had created than she had been herself. "Good-bye . . . soldier," she said. She climbed into the vehicle and settled behind the wheel, looking out across the desert. What the hell—life had been getting too soft. Time to begin again. She swung the vehicle around and drove off into the west, into the wasteland, the other vehicles following behind her.

Slowly Max dragged himself to his knees, staggered to his feet, only the pain of keeping his body upright proving to him that he had really survived. He stood numbly staring into the distance, smoke swirling around him, stinging his eyes. The plane was nothing but a silver speck in the heavens; Entity and the remains of her army were only a dust cloud fading into the west. He stood alone in the wreckage, staring after them until they had completely disappeared.

Jedediah flew on into the evening with no goal in mind now except a flat place to land before his fuel ran out. The thought of losing everything he owned and being pitched out into the wilderness by a total stranger, left with nothing but the clothes on his back, was one that caused him considerable grief. But then, considering the alternatives . . . He sighed, shrugging loose the last of the tension in his narrow shoulders as he looked over at his son. *Things could always be worse.*

Mr. Skyfish crouched between them, looking out in awe at the rolling mountains of cloud passing by below and all around them, masses of purple and white and gold. Flying was even more wonderful than he had dreamed. He watched the sunset flow around from his right as the plane banked, until its fiery reds and oranges lay directly ahead, framed in the cockpit's window.

The plane pitched and struggled through a pocket of rough air; Jedediah took it lower as they approached the cloudbank looming ahead. His fuel gauge was flirting with empty; time to start looking for flat ground.

Savannah and the others, still looking out the doorway, blinked in surprise and fascination as they plunged into the clouds, their view suddenly obscured by the cool, moist grayness of fog. The plane dropped lower and lower through the ocean of misty gray, until below them they saw the sky brightening again, a hole opening in the clouds.

As the plane dropped through the bottom of the clouds Jedediah saw the ground, saw an immense, broken canyon rushing up to meet them. Hastily he pulled the plane's nose up, leveling out just below the rim. Having no idea where he was and no better guide, he followed the twisting path of the canyon walls.

Ahead, the walls of the canyon curved, cutting off his vision. Banking sharply, he rounded the bend. Jedediah gaped in amazement. Ahead of him, vaulting out from the two rims of the canyon, were the separate ends of a mighty bridge—perfectly intact but with their entire center section missing. The two ends reached out toward each other in black silhouette, like two lovers' hands that would never touch again. What had once been a harbor was now a wide, dust-dry valley.

Jedediah brought the plane around, gaining altitude

again as they passed over one end of the bridge. Beyond it he saw the folded white wings of the once-famous Opera House, drifted with sand, its layered shell-form domes pocked with holes, resting now on the rim of a towering bluff instead of the harbor's shore. Beyond lay the city, the monolithic ruins of its buildings jutting like crystals from the encroaching desert sand, abandoned and silent, waiting. . . .

As Jedediah took the plane higher over the center city, weaving through the towering canyons of broken glass and twisted steel, Savannah stared down in speechless awe at the vision below them. It could only be Tomorrow-morrow-Land. She had dreamed of it all her life, and the reality was far more wonderful, more beautiful, more magical and shining than she had ever imagined it would be.

She looked down into the open top of a broken sky-scraper as the plane lifted suddenly, clearing its peak, dropping down again. They had reached the edge of the city; ahead of them now lay the ruins of the suburbs, a rolling plain lapped by creeping dunes. Jedediah began to take them down as a flat tongue of what had once been highway opened out in welcome below, blown clear of sand. At last they had really come Home. . . .

He hadn't been Walker; she was sure of it now. And yet he had saved them . . . had made everything come true just as the Tell had promised. The image of his face looking back at them for the last time, with an expression she had never expected to see in his eyes, filled her memory. She would never forget that look, or the truths he had taught her. She glanced over at Pig Killer and Master, past them at the Tribe. She would never let any of them forget. . . .

EPILOGUE

The wasteland lay waiting for him, as it had lain waiting for him for years, would lie waiting until eternity . . . vast and empty, its secrets slowly falling into shadow once more. The last light of the setting sun made stained glass of the western sky, amber and rose and violet, an unearthly purity of light illuminating the west as he slung the bedroll and water bottle at his back and picked up his gun. Limping painfully, he began to walk, not looking back, because there was nothing to look back after.

"This you knows," Savannah said, her voice ringing out across the firelit sea of faces. "I be First Tracker and times past count I done the Tell. But it ain't one body's Tell. It's the Tell of us all. And you gotta lissen it and 'member—'cos what you hears today, you gotta tell the birthed tomorrow. . . ." As she recited the words that she had spoken so many times, she looked out across the ruined city, its towers silhouetted against the star-hung, indigo sky. The lights of other fires, flickered here and there among the ruins. "I's lookin behind us now—into history back. . . . I sees those of us that got the luck and started the haul for home. And I 'members how it led us here and how we was heartfull—'cos we seen what there once was. . . . "

Here on this rooftop, so unimaginably high above the ground, so close to the sky, the gathered members of her own Tribe sat around a bonfire, listening as they had listened so often over the years to their story. There were nearly fifty of them now, most of them children, many her own. So many new faces. . . . Her eyes touched briefly, fondly, on the handful of faces that she had known from the beginning, their smiles mirroring the passage of years, mirroring the changes in her own face. "One look and we knowed we got it straight—those what had gone before had the knowin' and the doin' of things beyond our reckonin' . . . even beyond our dreamin'. . . . Time counts and keeps countin' and we knows now—findin' the trick of what's been and lost ain't no easy ride. But that's our track, we gotta travel it, and there ain't nobody knows where it's gonna lead. . . . "

She looked away from them again, into the flames, her gaze on something beyond reach, beyond sight. "Still and all, every night we does the Tell, so that we'll 'member who we was and where we came from. . . . But most of all we 'members the man who finded us, him that came the salvage. . . . " At her signal two of the Tribe moved forward to stoke the fire so that it blazed up like a beacon in the night. In the flames she could still see the face of the man she had sworn would never be forgotten, for as long as there were memories or words. "And we lights the beacons, but not just for him—for all of 'em that are still out there. . . ." She looked up again, away toward the desert, her voice rising, " 'Cos we knows there'll come a night when they sees the flickering light, and they'll be coming home. . . ."

He made his way along the crest of a ridge as the last fires of twilight faded into ashes, following the mesa's meandering course because all directions were the same in the wasteland. Walking the knife edge above a black shadow sea, lost in the darkness like a single star, he traveled alone, deeper into the night.